This page is intentionaly left blank.

Published by: Carnival of Glee Creations

Text Design by: William Allen Pepper

Cover Design by: William Allen Pepper

A CIP record for this book is acailable from the Library of Congress Cataloging-in-Publication Data

Paperback ISBN: 978-0-9818647-7-8

E-book ISBN: 978-0-9818647-8-5
Distributed by: Carnival of Glee Creations

William Allen Pepper

2ND DUCK ON THE RIGHT

AND

OTHER VERY SHORT STORIES

Carnival of Glee Creations

Dedicated to Jill, who is very patient.

Also by WILLIAM ALLEN PEPPER:

Hell's Cereal: Very Short Stories Fortified With Essential Syllables

Misery Banana: Very Short Stories Inspired by Old Games and Odd Thoughts

In the St. Nick of TIme (as William Pepper)

2ND DUCK ON THE RIGHT

AND OTHER

VERY SHORT STORIES

WILLIAM ALLEN PEPPER

SECOND DUCK ON THE RIGHT

"Shit," Billy Bisquin, seventh grader, said when his buddy Emily's turn at the "Plunk-a-Duck" was over. Again. With no prize.

The morning after Carson Carnival rolled into town, Emily Fallon got twenty dollars from her mother. She had burned through all but three of it on the "Plunk-a-Duck" shooting gallery. Those damn ducks just wouldn't fall.

"Hey, hey, language," Cal gently scolded. "This here's a family spot, you know." He chuckled a dry, raspy laugh. He didn't have a cigarette in his mouth, but likely there was one not far away.

Emily looked at Mr. Bird, a three-foot tall pink and gold stuffed toy parrot on the top prize shelf. Emily had earned enough tickets throughout the carnival before lunch to give her a shot – no pun intended – at winning the bird. All she had to do was take down the ducks in the shooting gallery.

Emily really wanted that bird.

She looked at the last three dollars in her hand. No way would she get more money from her mom, so this was it. And the Twist 'n' Dangle ride wasn't cheap. With a sigh, she told her friends, "Let's just go."

"Oh, man," Billy groaned. "I thought you were gonna do it this time."

Brenda just shrugged. She really didn't care one way or another, frankly.

The three started to walk away. Cal saw his day's take ebbing, and the carney kicked it into gear.

"Hold on, hold on," Cal said. "Ladies…" with a nod to Billy, he added, "AND gentleman. Don't get discouraged."

"Aw, I heard this game was rigged anyway," Billy sneered.

"Billy…" Brenda scolded.

"Nah, it's cool," Cal said. "People say stuff like that all the time. But the truth is," he squinted intently and pointed at each of the kids. "The truth is, it's a tough game. Don't feel bad. I been doing this a long time, and I've only known one kid who could do it."

Cal got a dreamy look in his eye, staring off into space…or into the deep-fried-things-stand where Greta was doing amazing things with a pickle. Man, Cal loved Greta.

Emily and her friends were halfway to the Twist 'n' Dangle when Cal snapped out of his reverie and called them back.

"You're not giving up already, are you?" Cal said.

Emily shrugged. "Gotta go, mister."

"Come on," Cal said. "One more try?"

Emily looked at her friends. Brenda shrugged.

Billy was all like, "I wanna ride the puke rocket."

But Emily didn't like giving up.

As if reading her mind, Cal said, "You know, I knew another kid like you. He didn't want to give up neither."

Emily took a few steps back toward the "Plunk-a-Duck" stand. "You did?" she said.

Cal scratched at his white-whiskered chin. "Second duck on the right. That's what did you in, eh?

Emily glanced at the faded blue duck in the third row, second from the right. Chips of paint from age and better shots than Emily splayed across the duck's wing. The duck's smile wasn't faded though. Darn it.

Cal walked up to the duck, flicked away a speck of chipped paint. Then he turned to the kids standing by the line of air rifles. "Brent was a crack shot with an air rifle," he said.

"Brent?" Emily said.

"Yeah. It was my first year with the carnival," Cal said. "Ooh. That was a long time ago. I started my career mopping puke off the landing pad below the Twist 'n' Dangle, but I used to spend my breaks on the midway. I'd grab a corn dog and watch the barkers hustle the crowd."

Brenda was confused. "Hustle?"

"So, it is a trick," Billy said. "I knew it."

Cal smiled, gestured widely. "No, my friends. Games of chance, all. None more so than the shooting gallery. And there was one kid better than the rest. Propane or air, BB or buck shot, Stan had been to every carnival that ever showed up in the county from the time he could see over the railing of the shooting gallery booth. And from the time he could lift the air rifle, it was as natural as, I dunno, one of you kids with a game joystick or something."

"What's a joystick?" Billy said.

Before Cal could answer, Emily asked, "So, what did he do? Stan?"

"Do?" Cal asked.

"About the ducks."

"Oh. Right," Cal said. "Anyway, this one day, Stan spent like an hour on the Plunk-a-Duck and every time, that same duck …" Cal paused and pointed at the second duck on the right. "This one. That same duck stymied Stan every time."

"So what did he do?" Emily asked again.

"Well…" Cal said. "I don't know if I should tell you that." There was a twinkle in his eye. "I mean, you did quit and all."

Emily looked at her friends. Billy looked impatient. Brenda just looked bored.

Emily slapped down her last three dollars.

In a fluid gesture, Cal scooped up the three bills, reset the guns and the ducks Emily had managed to hit in her prior go round. "All right. Back in the saddle. Good for you."

"Wait," Billy said. "You gotta tell her how that kid Stan beat the ducks."

"You promised," Brenda said, suddenly engaged.

"So I did," Cal said. "Well…here's what happened. And I'm still amazed by this. I…no, it's too crazy. You can't do it."

"What. What?" Emily said, leaning forward.

"You promised," Billy repeated.

"Okay,' Cal said. "Stan stepped up to the railing, picked up the air rifle. Took aim. And…closed his eyes and pulled the trigger."

"Closed his eyes?" Brenda said, displaying previously unknown depths of incredulity. "He shot a gun with his eyes closed?"

Cal waved his hands. "I know. It sounds crazy. But Stan…the determination in that boy's eyes…

well, seeing that stoney face made me drop my frozen banana. It was something. That boy believed he could hit that duck more than any person has ever believed anything. He was determined. He felt it." Cal paused for effect. "And you can feel it too. I know you can."

'Wow," Emily said, despite herself.

"Oh come on," Brenda said, enjoying her new-found attitude.

Emily, though, gritted her teeth, picked up the air rifle and took aim.

Cal, for his part, stepped well off to the side of the shooting range.

Emily closed her eyes and fired. Once. Twice. Three times.

She didn't come close to hitting anything.

The three kids left, maybe three levels smarter, but certainly three dollars poorer.

Cal, even on a slow mid-week, rainy day at the carnival, was three dollars richer.

And the universe was as it always has been.

"I still get me cut, right?" said the second duck on the left.

"Of course. Same split as usual."

Inspired by ATARI BYTES episode 220: CARNIVAL. The podcast is the audio equivalent of carnival food on sticks.

THE SORCERER'S RETIREMENT

The cake at Gant's retirement party was store bought. Though the icing was personally conjured by Isabelle in the Spells Receivable department, the writing on top spelled out "Happy Retirement, GRANT" is bold, red letters.

Gant had worked for the company for one-hundred-forty-three years. No one noticed the intruding "R" in his name.

No one but Gant. He didn't say anything though.

Then, that's how things usually went around here.

Gant sat back and brushed cake crumbs from his beard. In a bit of revenge, he'd managed to snag the piece with the "R" on it. He brushed thoughtfully at his flowing beard as he looked around at his coworkers. They were so young. That was a cliché, wasn't it? They're getting younger all the time.

No, Gant, he thought. You're getting older. Which was also a cliché, but seemed all the more depressing for it. It was flippant, but also devastatingly true.

The up-and-coming male sorcerers still wore beards, as they most always had, but they were shorter, more manicured facial art. All manner of trimmers and oils and special soaps and what not were applied. Too much fuss, it seemed to Gant, was put into those beards, as it was into a lot of things.

Back in his day – ugh, another cliché – sorcerers just got on with their sorcery. Evil wizard threatening to destroy the kingdom? Go to work. Hell's demons bent on world domination? Send them back from whence they came. A tear in the fabric of reality? Seal that mother f-er up. No need to face time other sorcerers about it or take a Twitter poll or wring one's hands over the unfairness of the intrusion. Just grab your wand and fix the problem.

That's why he was retiring, Gant supposed. The simplicity of how he got things done was out of step with modern wizardry.

Eshton, a young buck no more than sixty or so, took the seat next to Gant at the conference table; paper plate in one hand, utensil in the other. "Gant, man," Eshton said, gesturing with the fork like a wand, long nose pointed in Gant's direction, "Congrats. What you gonna do now?"

Gant half smiled. "Well, I suppose first I'll clean out my laboratory. Do you have any need of some magical pinecone?"

Eshton laughed. "You still have that? I thought the regenerative properties of pinecone were debunked years ago."

"Don't believe everything you hear."

Eshton shook his head. "I guess it's just an old guard thing. The apprentices now days get taught more about sumac than pine. Times change, I guess."

Gant shrugged. Maybe times did change. He did not. Gant reached for another piece of cake; this one had a blue flower drawn in the icing, or possibly a bird? No, it was definitely a castle.

Eshton pushed away from his own cake plate, no more than two bites into his first piece. "I'm stuffed," he said. "Gotta keep in top form, right?" He patted his abs and stood, thrusting a hand at Gant, who accepted it, if reluctantly. "Good luck. Smooth sailing, man," Eshton said and bounded away.

Gant enjoyed being with his cake a bit before Camilla approached and stood behind him. He sensed her presence, yes, but mostly he was caught in the haze of the many scents she wore. The smell resulting from nature's odors stacked one upon another was not unpleasant, just…olfactorily exhausting.

"Hello, Camilla," Gant said without turning around.

Camilla's calm voice emanated from deep within herself. Or perhaps from within all of time and space. It was difficult to tell. "Gant," she said, "like the wizards of Carmox who stepped back into the light after decades in the valley of the dark times, holding at bay the celestial spiders, you are poised upon the threshold of a new adventure."

"Well, really, I'm just going 'cause the retirement fund matured, Camilla."

Camilla nodded. "The wizards of Carmox, too, used their resources to reshape the world left asunder by the nightmare reign that came before. What will you, Gant, do with your resources?"

Gant shrugged. "I was considering buying a lake cabin."

Camilla nodded approvingly. "Real estate is a good investment." She glided away slowly, melding into the print on the wall of skydivers in freefall, holding hands above the caption 'Teamwork'. As she glided through the photo, Camilla put parachutes on all the divers which opened in a rainbow of color; the divers floated to the ground before Camilla disappeared and the skydivers returned to their original positions.

Gant considered going back to his office to finish cleaning out the magical, three-tailed winstril cages. Winstrils had long since gone extinct in the wizarding world; though they were genetically prone to invisibility and clouding human perception of them, putting an asterisk next to the extinction determination.

Before he could get up and go do that, Gant felt the rolling office chair next to him bump his knee. He looked around and saw no one. From below the table, Gant heard a small voice: "Please, sir," the voice said. "A little help…?"

Gant looked down into the hopeful, but sort of confused, face of Syl, the child wizard recently discovered having a tantrum in the toothpaste aisle of a discount store. In her rage – cause unknown – she caused the smiling, shiny faces on the toothpaste tubes to go on a biting rampage. The company recruited her right away, hoping to hone her skills for good. Syl, for her part, just hoped wizarding would stop her mom from making her take piano lessons.

"Little help, sir?" Syl said again.

Gant, with a grunt, reached down and lifted Syl up into the chair beside him. "Thanks," she said.

The little girl glowed with the radiance of other-worldly power. Gant remembered that glow; the glow he had nowadays was more from sorcerer-grade hemorrhoid cream.

"What's retirement?" the girl asked before tucking into the large piece of cake that appeared before her.

Gant considered this before saying, "The end of one's professional life," he finally said.

"Oh," Syl said. "So, you're dying." She took a big bite out of a frosting letter "T" from the cake.

"Not...exactly," Gant said. "Well, I mean, we all are, I guess."

"Not me," Syl said, shaking her head vigorously. "I'm a lastamorph."

"Good for you." Lastamorphs were immortals. And usually snotty about it. It bothered Gant a little that lastamorphs even got pension funds. Why did they need to retire?

"That means you'll be dead while I'm still young," Syl said. A field of tombstones illuminated with magical lightning appeared on the table, then faded away like the wizards who lay beneath them.

"So it seems," Gant said.

"Well, bye," Syl said, hopping down from the chair. "I gots to go push back the armies of the underworld." Syl skipped away.

Gant looked around and sighed. His coworkers gradually slipped away; a few stopped to shake his hand. Others escaped with a half wave or maybe calling over, "Good luck," or something. One even said, "We'll miss you, Grant," but Gant was pretty sure he was lying.

Gant looked around the empty room. He created a mini snowstorm from the sheet cake crumbs and bits of icing on the plate in the center of the table.

As the crumbs finally settled, Gant muttered to himself, "Armies of the underworld, eh?" Officially, today was Gant's last day of work, but he still had weeks of paid leave, so technically he was still employed with the company. And there was no way that short little lastamorph Syl could even see out the window of the wizarding transport, much less repel the armies of the underworld.

That lake cabin would just have to wait.

Inspired by Atari game "Sorcerer's Apprentice" from ATARI BYTES episode 206, despite having nothing to do with that famous cartoon mouse. Also, I'm a fan of cake.

THE INFINITE CIRCUS

On the outskirts of the galaxy, the fourth moon of a dead planet sits, devoid of all noise. Not even so much movement as a gust of wind disrupts the soulless landscape.

You might be surprised to know that before Imperial President Blarg rerouted the galactic highway as a favor to business interests, the planet and moons above were quite busy indeed. After Blarg's impeachment on corruption charges, mandatory cryogenic freezing and launching into the next galaxy with nothing to listen to but singles from failed Martian indie rockers, a bill was introduced in the galactic senate that would have created an off ramp for the planet. The planet's government at that time still had citizens with some clout – i.e. credits to spend – and wanted bodies to patronize their businesses. The bill was defeated, however, when Senate Leader Mooshoo tripped on a tentacle and died from the resulting head injury.

The new senate leader had once been served runny eggs in a diner on the planet's surface and his ill will killed the bill.

But back in the day, the fourth moon was home to the Infinite Circus. This was the premiere – or so it claimed – venue for marvelous acts of all kinds. Tight rope walkers. Fire eaters. Giant cars inserting themselves into tiny clowns. But the circus, like everything else on the planet, couldn't survive without revenue and it eventually closed; gradually falling into disrepair and mingling with the planetary dust.

Back in the day, the star attraction at the Infinite Circus was the legion of birdback riders; skilled riders who emerge out of the sedentary mists of the east astride massive, winged beasts. You might call them ostriches, but they would be insulted. The beasts, extinct now, for so goes the Infinite Circus so goes the company, were called Tawmads and had long legs, great, flowing wings and row upon row of feathers, streaked forest green and umber. Their large eyes conveyed a perpetual air of disdain and they were, frankly, jerks. The birdback riders had to be fearless, well-trained, and extraordinarily patient.

As a result, the birdback riders – birdbackers - tended to be jerks themselves. A defense mechanism perhaps

As the circus neared its peak, just before the end times, there was no bigger birdbacker – or bigger jerk – than Colin.

"Hey," Colin would say as the circus' other big draw Eleanor rode in on her bird, "Who let the sidesaddle in here?"

Eleanor did indeed ride sidesaddle atop Moondust. She did this because her costume was mostly made of tin – for complicated reasons – and it was difficult to straddle the bird. Whenever Colin would shout this, both Moondust and Eleanor would shake their heads dismissively and Eleanor would shout back, "Got to ride sidesaddle. I've got more down there to protect than you."

Then Colin would laugh and grunt to his bird, Mystery, "Girls, man."

Both Colin and Eleanor had served as knights in the galactic federation. Colin liked to tell war stories at night in the bunkhouse after the last performance. Eleanor liked to contradict him.

"Did I ever tell you boys about the time I liberated Kephalon from the Blarg with just my fists and Mystery's flatulence?" he'd say to the other performers.

"I hope not," Eleanor would say from her bunk across the room. "Because you were never on Kephalon. I assigned you to kitchen duty on Phasma."

By the way, during the war, Eleanor was Colin's commanding officer.

Then Colin would whisper to the others, "Well, don't say nothin', but I had secret assignments from higher up."

"No, you didn't," Eleanor would call over. She had really good hearing.

After the war, Colin was immediately drawn to the glitz of the Infinite Circus. He wowed the owners with his reckless abandon and Mystery's speed. They could do barrel rolls and other tricks that would make most birds barf, if not explode their brains. Mystery possessed unheard of genetic thrust vectoring that allowed him to do amazing things…which Colin was happy to take credit for.

"That bird would be on a bun with some fries and a cola at a fast-food joint if it wasn't for me," Colin would say.

Eleanor's journey to the Infinite Circus was a little more circuitous. After a particularly nasty firefight on Okana XIIII, she retired from the galactic federation with full honors. She tried private consulting but found the mixture of military and money distasteful. And being a talking head on the news channels felt…empty. Civilian jobs were no more fulfilling. How could she go from putting her life on the line for the galaxy, a life of service for other people, to a life of serving to other people…be it food, insurance or footwear?

Eleanor attended the Infinite Circus with her niece one afternoon and was immediately intrigued. Not in love, mind you, but intrigued. She could never quite explain why she decided to sign up – she joked having to continue paying for Moondust's chow herself was too much of a burden – but sign up she did and never looked back.

Until the circus closed, that is. Before that last show, though he'd never admit it, Eleanor found Colin weeping in the colloquially named bird barn, hanging for dear life from Mystery's neck. Even the bird looked sad.

"Shut up, Sidesaddle," Colin grunted when Eleanor walked in. "I wasn't crying."

"I didn't say anything," Eleanor responded.

"Whatever," Colin said. "You ready to do this?"

"We went over the routine, Colin," Eleanor said. "I'll hit my marks."

"Nah. Not that. You ready, you know, for what's

after…" he gestured wildly with his arms. "…
what's after the circus."

"Oh," Eleanor said. "I mean, sure." But her eyes
said otherwise.

"Yeah," Colin said, avoiding eye contact. "Me
too."

That day's performance was the best attended
since the Infinite Circus opened an infinitely long
time ago. Back then, the attendees were mostly
weirdly-attentive, single-celled organisms and
time travelers. Turns out, there are a LOT of time
travelers around.

Anyway, after the final show, the circus ringmas-
ter thanked the audience for its support and bid
them farewell. Then he deflated and slithered out
of the center ring.

The question on the performers' minds, of course,
as they loaded up the train for their last journey,
was: What happens to them?

"We're the infinite circus," said the tired old ring-
master to the now ex-performers assembled under

the soon-to-be-collapsed big top. He had aged even since the last performance; much like insects he only lived a few days. He lifted his top hat from his head and ruffled his hair. "And remember, nothing that's infinite really goes away."

"Tell that to my paycheck," Colin called back to scattered, forced laughs.

And with that, the big top folded in on itself, forcing the now unemployed performers to scatter. They say you can't fold something more than a finite number of times, but the Infinite Circus, by definition, was not limited to the merely finite. The circus – all the tents, the equipment, the concessions and the performers were folded into…well, no one really knows. The infinite circus, and the last of the species of Tawmads, for all practical purposes, simply disappeared. The ultimate center ring attraction and no one was there to see it.

Except…

After the new bypass was finally built and traffic to the planet resumed, the inevitable development plans sprung up. Luxury resorts, restaurants, gaming venues and cities around them for the workers to live in spread across the planet once again like the rash Colin once got after a night of drunken partying on Blorton.

One night, seven-year-old Oswald, vacationing with his folks who came for the Galaxy Metal Thrash Orchestra concert, awoke. He went to the window of his hotel room and, though sleepy, was certain he saw…a huge bird soar across the moon, one of them anyway.

In the distance, there was music.

Inspired by "Joust" from episode 207 of ATARI BYTES. For all the scorn heaped upon circuses, they sure inspire a lot of literature, don't they? Also, stories like the stuff I write.

CENT-IMPEDED

It's 1990. Nelson Mandela is released from prison. Margaret Thatcher resigns as UK prime minister. Milli Vanilli is caught cheating. Forced to give up their Grammys, they might soon be washing windshields for pennies. This would be a problem, especially if certain revolutionaries got their way…

Passers-by in that small Arizona town might have

noticed, if they cared to look, the dingy glow from a sodium light spilling out onto the sidewalk through a basement window of The Curated Collectibles, the town's only collectible and hobby shop.

In the basement-turned-war-room, the shop's owner, Sonata Lovelace, stood uneasily at one end of the ping-pong-table-turned-conference-table. For the third time in five minutes, she readjusted the scrunchie holding her ponytail.

At the opposite end of the table, Fletcher flinched when the overhead light's reflection played off of Sonata's reproduction of "the one ring to rule them all". He ducked under the table.

Sitting between the two, Constance Midway's eyeroll looked painful. "There are no pennies down here, Fletcher. You know the rule. No coin shooting allowed."

Fletcher cautiously sat up. He was a life-long target of errant penny flicking and would take no chances.

"Can we get on with this, please?" Constance said.

"Yes. Right," Sonata responded, adjusting her ponytail and her posture, befitting the leader of a revolution; for a revolution it was. These three, along with a small army, most of whom couldn't make it tonight, you know 'cause of work and stuff. Oh, and the final part of Ken Burns Civil War mini-series was on that night and some of them wanted to get home to see how it would end.

So, for now, it was just Sonata, Constance and Fletcher leading the charge. That is, the charge to eradicate the penny from U.S. currency.

"Our mission," Sonata said. "Is to see the cent impeded." She chuckled. No one else did.

"You know, like the old Atari game, CENTI-PEDE?"

Blank stares. Constance and Fletcher were a bit younger than Sonata. It showed.

"Anyway," Sonata continued. "I just got word that Congressman Kolbe's Price Rounding Act has been…defeated."

Fletcher pumped his fist. "Yes! I can afford some

Air Jordans now."

"No, Fletcher, I said H.R. 3761 is dead."

"Oh, Fletcher said. "Which one is that?"

"The bill to eliminate the penny in cash transactions. Instead, retailers would have to round to the nearest nickel."

"I told you it would never pass," Constance said, yawning. "Why do we hate the penny again?"

"Because, Constance," Sonata said, "you can't buy anything for a penny anymore. It's wasted currency. When's the last time you bought a penny gumball? Everything is out of control. I hear gasoline might go over a dollar a gallon."

"One-a-penny, two-a-penny. Hot cross buns," Fletcher said. The other two just stared at him.

"That's England, Fletcher," Sonata said. "They're not like the U.S. They don't have political problems."

"What's the big deal?" Constance said. "You don't like pennies? Put them in the bank. Use them as weights in stuff like draperies. I whacked my brother in the head the other day – he knows what he did – and he even made a cold compress out of some pennies."

Sonata vibrated visibly. "The productivity drain in the workplace from having to take time to count all those pennies is staggering."

"One…two…three…four," Fletcher demonstrated. He didn't have any pennies, so he used Pez candies from one of his Garfield dispensers instead. Purple ones. He looked proud of himself.

"Plus," Sonata said, "zinc is a main component in pennies and zinc is really lethal."

"It's true," Fletcher said. "The last time a ton of zinc fell on my grandpa…well, it was kinda the first time too, I guess. Flat as a pancake. But, you know, some Tylenol and he was good to go. 'till the steamroller. They played Looney Tunes cartoons at his funeral. Don't know why."

"Anyway…point is," Sonata said. "The penny

has to go. Retailers can just round to the nearest nickel." She irritably flicked a paper clip across the table. Fletcher shuddered.

"Sticking it to customers in the process, and thereby aiding the process," Constance said through a smirk.

"Congressman Kolbe's bill said they would have to round down," Sonata said.

"That bill that didn't pass," Constance said. "So what's the next move?" Another yawn.

That's where the piece of college-ruled notebook paper with the fringed edges Sonata was holding ran out. She didn't know what was next. Was all this a crazy notion? Why did she hate the penny so much? Lincoln had been on the penny since 1909. She had no grudge against him. President Polk, though…what a douche bag.

A flash of purple lightning bathed the room in a blueberry glow – seriously, blueberries look purple, weird.

"It's fourth grade all over again," Fletcher

screamed, diving under the ping pong table.

The lightning dissipated. A man stood on the ping-pong table looking down at Sonata and Constance with a self-satisfied smile. He wore a trucker hat, boot-cut jeans and a holographic shirt, like if Obi-Wan Kenobi was a dead jedi who came back as a shirt that said Nike on it instead of as a Force Ghost.

"Fear not the penny," the man said.

"Uh…," was the best Sonata could come up with.

"I am the future," the man said, then cleared his throat. "Sorry. I meant, I'm from the future."

"Like, next week?" Fletcher called from below the ping-pong table.

"A little further than that," the man said. "The twenty-first century."

"And the penny is dead!" Sonata said triumphantly.

"Nope," the man said. "Sorry to disappoint. The penny is alive, but pretty useless. Like mail carriers. In the future, we've got something better."

"What do you mean?" Sonata said.

The man put both hands in his back pockets, then flicked them forward, like a gunslinger brandishing his six-shooters. In one hand, he held a debit card.

"Oh, an ATM card, "Constance said. "That's creative. Good luck finding an ATM machine."

The man shrugged. In the other hand, he had a fistful of gold coins, which he flung outward. Unfortunately, Fletcher had just emerged from under the table and took the brunt of shrapnel.

"What are those?" Sonata said. "They don't look like pennies."

"Bitcoin!" the man said proudly. Money that exists entirely on the computer."

The three revolutionaries looked confused. Sonata

pointed. "But it's right there," she said. "You just threw it."

"Nah, that's just for show. Bitcoin is only money on the computer. You can't carry it around with you."

"Oh," Sonata said. "How do you get it?"

"You have to buy it," the man said. "With physical money."

"Then what?"

"Well, then you use bitcoin to buy stuff and pay people like you would normally. Just on computer."

"Why?" Sonata said.

"It's easier," the man said.

"Last week, I tried to download a file I needed for my graduate thesis," Constance said. "I'm still waiting for it to finish."

"So, I never get to put bitcoin in my pocket?" Sonata said.

"Nope," the man said. "Not unless you buy it back with regular money."

"Why couldn't I have just used regular money to begin with?"

"Uh…"

"The future is weird," Constance said.

"You have no idea," the man said.

Inspired by ATARI BYTES episode 208: CENTIPEDE for the Atari 7800 this time. The game hos nothing to do with money. Spoilers.

BAD POETRY CORNER:

THE SWEET SCIENCE IN A WORLD THAT HATES SCIENCE: A POEM

The crowd does murmur in joyful

Popcorn prelude to the fervor

That awaits as lights go up.

In the ring, opponents square off.

Silence engulfs, save for one cough.

Never mind a pin,

You can hear the sweat drop.

Spectators lean in and

Aboard the discord wagon hop.

On social media, "debate" is just retorts.

Violence becomes yet another sport.

Climate abuse of all sorts.

Health care does our cash extort.

Go ahead, throw a punch.

Then look to see where it lands.

On folks I dislike, well, there's a bunch.

Culture fractured into competing bands.

"I know what I know," people say.

Even when science goes the other way.

Society fights and scorns so much

Corrupt power lorded over us.

Social media shouts loud and proud.

Digital character fists thrown freely.

'till opponents we verbally pound.

Does revenge make me greedy?

Oh, right, but what of those boxers in the ring?

Punch drunk with their power.

We watch from outside, happy to sing

Glad some are behind the scenes to cower.

It's fight night again.

Let the struggle begin.

Or, you know, just walk away.

Live to fight another day.

Inspired by ATARI BYTES episode 209: FIGHT NIGHT for the Atari 7800.

DONKEY DESTINY

(Thanks to John Mellencamp for no particular reason…)

A little poem 'bout a Jack and a Jennie

Two donkeys (or burros or asses) growing up where it's warm

The jack, he's gonna be feral and wild

But the jennie'll stay with a Mideast herd for a while

Chowin' down on grass and shrubs, pull with their lips not their teeth

Bodies use up most of what they eat;

Not much poop there to see

The Jack, he says:

"Hey, Jennie, let's run off with some zebras

Maybe find us some willing horses

Raise up some mules who will love us.

Braying, oh yeah…

Donkey life goes on, long after the thrill of herd living is gone

Brayin', oh yeah…

Donkey life goes on, long after the thrill of herd living is gone

Now load your pack on…

Jack, he sits back, flops his ears in thought for a moment

Scratches some fleas, and does his best bad ass routine.

"Well, now, then, Jennie, we ought to protect livestock from predators."

Jennie says:

"Baby, you ain't missing nothing."

But the Jack, he brays:

"Oh yeah. Donkey life goes on – can be more than 40 years long."

"But not for the wild asses. All endangered; almost gone."

"Oh, watch out for rocks in the field, don't go for a roll."

"May our sense of safety save our souls."

"Holdin' on to our sense of direction long as we can."

"The farmer will come 'round at noon"

"With some grass in a pan."

Oh yeah, donkey life goes on…

A little poem 'bout a Jack and a Jennie,

Two kind-hearted beasts of burden doin' the best that they can…

Inspired by ATARI BYTES episode 210, DONKEY KONG for the Atari 7800. And, of course, my rock star soul.

PERFECT MATCH

Gary watched, both amused and horrified, as Josh drained the pint glass of IPA in one go. As he set the glass on the table, Josh's hand, ring on each finger, twitched a bit. The glass thudded on the table, but didn't break.

"That cost me six bucks," Gary said. "You could have at least tasted it."

The rings on Josh's fingers clacked nervously

against the tabletop. His eyes were wide as he stared through the neon "BEER" sign out the window to the sidewalk. Whenever someone walked by, he jumped, sending the Naugahyde under his butt into paroxysms.

"What is with you, man?" Gary said. "What was with those texts about someone following you?"

"Shhhhh!" Josh hissed. He leaned toward the window and scanned. "Is that…?"

Gary's beefy arm gently pulled his friend back down into the seat. "What is the deal?"

After ordering another round – and making short work of it – Josh finally spilled it.

"A tiny man is following me."

Gary chewed a hot wing for a moment as he pondered this. Then, "A tiny man?"

"Yeah," Josh said, still staring out the window. "Only, he's not so much a little man as a sort of… bowling pin-shaped creature."

"I like bowling," Gary said. "Wanna bowl a few frames tonight?"

"Can't," Josh said. "The little man with the bowler hat is trying to kill me."

"I thought you said he was bowling pin shaped; not that he was wearing a bowler hat."

"He's both. And he wants to kill me."

"Really?"

"I mean…probably?" Josh said. "Every time I turn around. There he is. Just grinning."

"So, he's friendly?" Gary said. "That's something, right?"

Josh smirked. "Friendly like in a 'Why does he want to kill you' way?"

"Look, I'm just trying to keep up," Gary said.

Halfway through his third IPA, Josh shrugged. "I don't know. All he ever says is, 'I'm your perfect match."

Gary inhaled another boneless wing. "What's that mean?"

Josh's intestines clutched as he barely suppressed a shriek. "I'm about to find out. Here he comes" The glasses on the table toppled as Josh bolted from the bar.

Gary calmly finished his wings. "He's kind of messed up," he muttered.

Outside, Josh bounced off a lime green Tesla as he bolted into a side alley.

It was an alley that led to a really tall brick wall. Like in a movie. Josh was about to turn back, wondering how he could steal the Tesla and get away. Would you hot wire it like a gas-powered car? It's electric which meant wires, he supposed, so yeah.

While Josh was posed in a fighting stance, distracted with the mechanics of green technology theft, the creature stepped between his legs.

Suddenly aware of a presence, Josh glanced down. A small man with the smile of a Cheshire cat and the body of a bowling pin, tipped his hat at Josh. "We're a perfect match," the creature said.

Josh gulped hard. The fighting stance, it turned out, was just for show.

"We're a perfect match," the creature said again.

Josh shook his head softly. "We don't…we don't look anything alike."

The bowling pin man cocked his head. It looked weird. "But we are a perfect match. I was made for you."

"Um, I don't think so…"

The bowling pin man put his hat back on. "You ever met a guy who looked like me before?"

"No."

"Then how do you know I wasn't made for you?"

"Uh....

"You should pick me up," the bowling pin man said.

"But I barely know you," Josh said, his brain doing the backstroke across a sea of confusion.

"I'm your perfect match."

"So you said."

"You need me. I was made for you," the bowling pin said, arms outstretched, waiting to be picked up.

"No freakin' way," Josh said.

And that's when Gary caved Josh's head in with a sixteen-pound, chartreuse bowling ball. He dropped the ball and it rolled into the side of a dumpster. Gary went looking for more wings.

As Josh crumpled in a surprised, bloody heap, the bowling pin man shrugged. "Josh could have used me," he said sadly. "We were a perfect match."

Inspired by the Atari game CONCENTRATION from ATARI BYTES episode 211. The game, of course, is a matching game, but has nothing to do with bowling. But, then, the story doesn't really either. If you listen to the show for any time at all, you find that's not really a requirement.

GET BACK, GAMMON!

The hazelnut latte at the Coffee Nut Hut on 43rd was just okay. Not as good as it was at the Coffee Nut Hut on Myrtle Boulevard, but that was across town and, besides, whenever Bryce Gammon found himself on that end of town at that Coffee Nut Hut, he had to get the white chocolate because theirs was to die for. The brownies were better too. Something about fresher walnuts maybe?

Anyway, the Coffee Nut Hut on 43rd was all right ("all right in a sort of a limited way for an off-night", Thank you, Mr. Paul Simon). But if the hazelnut latte was just all right, Chad the barista was AMAZING. Bryce was pretty sure he was already in a relationship, but whatever. The coffee was still pretty good. And sometimes Chad threw in a scone (or two!) for free.

You ever do that thing where you think of yourself in the third person? Like former U.S. Senator Bob Dole? You're doing it now, right? After looking up Bob Dole. Well, Bryce Gammon was doing it too. "Bryce Gammon likes the whipped," he muttered to himself as he took in the generous dollop of whipped cream on his beverage. Bryce also had a tendency not only to think of himself in the third person, but also to use both first and last names. He should ask Bryce Gammon's therapist about that.

"You were a little late today, Gammon," Chad said as he brushed some biscotti crumbs off the counter. "Missed you earlier."

Bryce Gammon's already caffeinated heartbeat pounded faster. He liked the way Chad referred to him by his last name. Made him feel cool in a way he most definitely was not. "Sorry. Off schedule today. I had a…dog thing." Bryce Gammon's labradoodle Marco had been having intestinal problems.

"Had to dump a hazelnut that was waiting for you

'cause it got cold," Chad said, smiling.

Bryce Gammon couldn't tell if Chad was teasing. It was stressful.

To make things worse, Chad's eyes – hazel, like Bryce's preferred coffee – went wide as he pointed with a trembling finger at something behind Bryce.

"What's wrong, Chad?" Bryce said.

"GET BACK, GAMMON!"

"Whu - ?" Bryce started to say before the wind rushed out of him as he was slammed to the floor. He felt hot breath on his neck as some creature panted above him.

Chad leapt over the counter and with a grunt, pulled the beast off of Bryce Gammon. "Shoo," he said. "Go on now."

Bryce stood on shaky feet, catching only a glimpse of a tail rounding the corner of the Coffee Nut Hut. Was that a big dog? A lion? "What was it?"

he asked.

Chad paused. "I'm not at liberty to say."

Bryce blinked a bit. "Um…what?"

"GET BACK, GAMMON!" Chad shrieked again, slamming Bryce to the floor himself this time. Bryce rolled over just in time to see Chad's beefy arms swatting away a swarm of vampire bats. Each one wore a tiny cape and carried a stir-stick sized machete. An unimpressed biscotti baker covered in hair and baking flour casually opened a window so the bats could fly out.

"You okay, Bryce Gammon?" Chad said.

"What the hell is going on here?" Bryce Gammon asked. "I mean sorry, sorry. But I don't understand…"

"Confusion?" Chad said seriously. "You sure those bats didn't bite you?"

"Yeah. Yeah. I'm sure."

"How are your feet? Any swelling? Can you still feel your penis? Any sudden urges to eat humans?"

"I'm FINE," Bryce Gammon said, owning the irritation now. "Tell me what all this –"

"GET BACK, GAMMON," Chad yelled.

Here we go again.

"Allow me," Bryce Gammon said and put himself on the floor just in time for a herd of three-headed llamas to stampede through the shop. Tables and chairs scattered in every direction. The rack of today's newspapers was shredded. The espresso maker clattered to the floor with a clatter and a hiss, steam filling the room.

Once the lamas had gone out the back, Chad helped Bryce Gammon up. "Crazy, huh?' he said.

"Those lamas had three heads," Bryce said.

"Not as weird as the machete bats though, am I right?" Chad said.

"Tell. Me. What. Is. Going. On." Bryce Gammon hissed. He was having trouble liking Chad right now.

Chad uneasily glanced at the biscotti baker who only shrugged. "Well, see the Coffee Nut Hut sits on top of a portal to a distant planet inhabited by exotic creatures. They're not supposed to, but once in a while some of them wander into the worm-hole and end up here. Chad smiled and held up his hands submissively. "Whoops."

Bryce Gammon looked around at the shambles of his favorite coffee shop. "But why…why would you…?"

"The rent was good," Chad explained.

"Good amount of off-street parking," the biscotti baker grunted, then appeared to go to sleep.

"Make sense?" Chad said.

Bryce Gammon wasn't sure if Chad was looking for an answer. He was equally unsure what that answer would be. "I better go. Marco has probably liquid-crapped on the carpet by now." Bryce, dazed, turn to leave.

"GET BACK, GAMMON," Chad yelled again.

"WHAT WHAT? PENGUINS WITH BAD B.O.? SNAKES WITH CLAWS? HOWLING SPIDERS? WHAT THE HELL IS IT?" Bryce screamed as he first set a table upright, then crawled under it.

"Oh. No," Chad said apologetically. "You just forgot your coffee."

Bryce Gammon stood and retrieved his cup.

"Know what. That one's on the house," Chad said.

"You bet your ass it is," Bryce Gammon mumbled.

Every day after that, Bryce Gammon set his alarm a little earlier so he could make it over to the Coffee Nut Hut on Myrtle Boulevard. It wasn't all bad. The barista Mitchell was hotter than Chad and the only creature encounters Bryce had to deal with was this one lady's schnauzer who liked to hump Bryce's ankles.

Oh, and Marco's intestinal problems have cleared up. The alien gut plumber that now lives in Marco's colon says 'hi'.

Inspired by BACKGAMMON from ATARI BYTES episode 212. If you think it's weird and a stretch, then you're starting to get the hang of how this works.

BAD POETRY CORNER:

ANATOMY OF VROOM: A POEM

The wheels on the bus go round and round.

Those wings make the planes take flight.

But when it comes to open wheel cockpit cars,

Just what makes Indy 500 out of sight?

The car's front wing and rear wing

They work together

Creating aerodynamic downforce

So the front and rear car work better

Two wing configurations

Speedway and road

Or road/street course and short oval

Too many options to ever get old

The chassis is the central part of the car

It includes a driver's compartment.

Other important stuff like

Anti-roll, brake cylinder and fuel vent.

The sidepod covers up the oil cooler

Can also benefit aerodynamics

Protects engine control unit and water radiator

And keeps the driver safe from crash dramatics

The fuel cell holds 18.5 gallons

It's totally made of rubber

Protected from side impacts

With a layer of Kevlar

Indy cars have assisted gear shifting

On the back of the wheel is the paddle shift system

The bellhouse connects the gearbox and engine
With parts like rear dampers and transmission

Chevy and Honda engines are 2.2 liter
The engine houses the oil tower,
Exhaust system and turbocharger
Surrounded by 550 – 700 horsepower

Firestone Firehawk racing radials
Eleven inches in front; fifteen in back
Mounted on 15-inch rims, they dissipate heat.
Ready for the stress of the track.

Front and rear – what holds them together?
Wheels attach to chassis by suspension.
Includes the brake discs, rear and front
Built to withstand braking and acceleration.

Round the track
All parts working as one
Finishing first is the goal
Never give up 'till the race is done.

Inspired by INDY 500 from ATARI BYTES episode 213. I have almost no idea what any of that poem means. Literary win!

PEANUT PUTTER BUTTER

Chuck "Monster Putter" Higgins leaned forward. With a grimace, he reached up with his right arm and tapped the "video" function of his teleconference software so that he could see what Charlotte was holding up.

The pain from yet another rotator cuff injury was unpleasant. These conference calls were worse.

"Right," Charlotte said. "Can you see this all right? I'll email it to you later. It's a mock-up of the label we'll be using on the jars."

"What's the grey patch in the middle?" Chuck asked.

"Oh, that's where the photo will go. We'll talk about that in a minute," Charlotte said.

"I told you I'm not doing a photo for the label," Chuck said.

"In a minute, silly," Charlotte giggled, a bit awkwardly. "So, we've settled on the name 'Monster Peanut Butter', right? We're going with that?"

Chuck didn't like how this was going. "Yeah, only I thought it was Monster Peanut Putter," Chuck said. "You know, like my nick name."

Charlotte smiled. The gap in her teeth was sort of endearing. "That's where this gets cool," she said. "If you like it, I can try to sell them on it. Look here…" Charlotte held up a second mock-up. This one had the lettering slightly different. "See," Charlotte explained," in this one, the wording is Monster Peanut Putter, with a 'P" but we've got the 'p" off center as a "B" shoves its way into the word with one of those, whadaycallit? Caret symbols." Charlotte thought for a moment. "Dunno if carrots and peanut butter go together, but, hey, so long as people buy it, right? They can smear it on whatever they like."

"No, wait, not carrot like the vegetable. The caret is spelled different," Chuck started to say, but didn't pursue it. Charlotte was enjoying her joke.

"I guess that's okay," he said, switching gears. "But what about the photo for the grey spot."

Charlotte made a please-don't-shoot-me face. "Oh, well, that's where the famous Chuck 'Monster Putter" Higgins' photo will go, of course," Charlotte said. "So, anyway…"

"Hold on," Chuck said. "We're not doing the costume thing you said last time, right?"

Charlotte chuckled. "But it's funny. Kind of whimsical. Not taking all this too serious. It's your trademark, right?"

Charlotte's argument was not without merit. Once during the Pebble Beach Pro-Am, Chuck had played each of the eighteen holes wearing a different pirate costume.

"Chuck the Monster Putter Butter Man. People will love it. There could be t-shirts. Merchandise. We'll make buttloads of cash off that while also promoting the peanut butter," Charlotte said.

"I'm not dressing up like a peanut to sell peanut butter, Charlotte," Chuck said. "That stuff is done.

I'm retired now."

Charlotte gently waved. "We'll stick a pin in that for now." She picked up her phone and looked at the time. "Shoot, I gotta go. So, I'll tell the graphics guys to jiggle with the font a bit – maybe something more nutty? I dunno. And I'll text you the details on the photo shoot."

"Charlotte…" Chuck started to say.

"Catch you later," Charlotte said and disconnected the call.

Chuck the Monster Putter Higgins sat back in his desk chair, which aggravated the herniated disk in his back. Bad shoulders and a bad back. It was hell to be old at forty. Sure, being old AND winner of all four major golf tournaments – The Masters, the U.S. Open, the British Open and the PGA Championship – helps, but still…

Chuck went downstairs in search of seltzer water. He wasn't sure why. Black cherry seltzer just sounded really good. The green jacket from the first Masters he won hung on the landing on a fancy wooden hanger that itself cost more than Chuck's first car. Chuck had never quite figured out what he was supposed to do with the jacket and this seemed as good an idea as any. As to why it hung on the landing, well, that's because, the night he won, still wearing the jacket, that was all the farther toward the bedroom he and his wife had gotten during their celebration.

Chuck wandered into the living room where a mannequin with some crazy plaid pants and wild hair wore the jacket from his second Masters. The mannequin was posed as if doing a hand-stand. Again, the Monster Putter wasn't sure if this showed the proper amount of reverence. This had never really bothered him though.

But it did kind of bother him now.

Chuck turned the mannequin right side up, but for this mannequin right side up was actually upside down. Its feet were flexed like one might when doing a handstand, unsuitable for standing flat-footed. The mannequin fell stiffly onto the couch, bounced lightly, then landed on the floor; the green of the jacket providing a splash of accent to the mahogany flooring.

Chuck's older daughter, Emily, came in from the driving range behind the house; phone in one hand, in the other hand a copy of the Monster Putter's book Teed Off…and Loving It!

"Hey, dude," Chuck said to Emily. "Saw you out there earlier. Make sure to keep your arm straight. You're still bending it a little."

"Yeah, thanks," Emily said, as she kept on walking.

"Hey, uh, you been reading my book?" Chuck asked.

Emily considered her answer. "Um, sort of…no," she said. "On the college visit yesterday, this guy's dad gave your book to Mom."

"Does he want my autograph?" The Monster Putter said.

"No, uh," Emily tried not to say. "He wanted a refund. And then he laughed. Only, he kind of wasn't laughing."

Chuck laughed , hearing a punchline that maybe wasn't there.

Emily set the book on the coffee table and skittered away. "Sorry, Daddy," she said as she left the room.

Chuck was pretty proud of that book. No ghost writer, even at his agent's urging. He resisted the original pitch – a coffee table book of wacky "Monster Putter" photos throughout the years. Instead, lots of practical golf advice. Some stories about growing up in Iowa. His philosophy of life. Okay, that part was a little harder. Chuck really did believe "give nice, get nice in return." But it sounded a little corny.

The book didn't sell great. Charlotte said it was market saturation or something.

Chuck wasn't sure. He really thought the style upgrade would work; sort of downplay the wacky and lean harder into the experienced athlete with things to say angle. He'd wanted to write another book. But now…well, he didn't know.

Can't golf. Can't write. He almost got a commentating gig for one of the networks airing the golf tournaments. He even made it to the screen test stage. But the network decided having the "Monster Putter" in the press booth undercut the seriousness of the event.

What should he do now?

Six months later, Monster Peanut Putter Butter came out in crunchy style.

The mannequin in Chuck's living room looks really good in Chuck's peanut costume.

Inspired by GOLF from ATARI BYTES episode 214. Insert hole-in-one joke here.

FIREWORLD FIRESALE

Mist swirled around the majestic columns and half-working neon lighting of the store known as FIREWORLD. One of those inflatable arm-flailing tube men stood guard. He didn't look like much; burnt orange stripes and an ear-to-ear grin that conveyed blank joy. But the eyes, though they never blinked, never even moved, still saw everything.

In the center of the Fireworld show room, Phillipe dozed lightly. Paperclips tangled in his beard as he lay head down on the desk. The sleeping angle ruined the line of his tailored, sparkly suit, but, well, it had been a slow day.

When the little bell over the door jingled, Phillipe startled and a few paper clips scattered to the floor, the rest left a rainbow chain in his beard.

At the sight of two new customers, Phillipe went into on-mode.

"Ladies!" Phillipe boomed, elegantly swiping away the paper clips. "Welcome to Fireworld, your one stop shop for fire from ember to conflagration. Our deals are hot!" He produced a golf-sized fireball that quickly extinguished. "How can I burn you today…in a good way?"

The two women, Madge and Constance, glowered down at the little salesman virtually prostrate before them. Madge turned to Constance and said, "We shouldn't be here. This wasn't on the shopping list." Her voice was piercing and awe-inspiring, but also the faintest whisper Phillipe couldn't be quite sure he'd heard.

"It's fine," Constance said. "Central office encourages spontaneity."

Madge snorted at that. "Central office isn't spontaneous. Central office is as predictable as the mortals' bowel movements."

Constance sighed. "Sir," she said to Phillipe. "We're under orders to obtain fire."

"No. We're not," Madge countered.

"Well, we weren't told not to," Constance said.

Phillipe beamed. "You've come to the right place." He gestured grandly around the empty show room. "We have everything from tasteful candlepower." At this point, a candelabra appeared and the wicks self-ignited. "All the way up to molten lava." The floor became a sea of magma then returned to normal just as quickly. "If you want to go big, we can provide awe-inspiring planetary devastation by flaming asteroid." The walls were engulfed in flame that immediately dissipated.

Madge was unimpressed.

"Well, our boss does like grand statements," Constance said.

"He likes water. Floods. Waves, storms," Madge said.

"He can't do water all the time," Constance said. "This will be better."

Constance turned back to Phillipe. "I guess what we're looking for is more…localized."

Phillipe nodded emphatically, though he didn't know what the hell they were talking about. "I see. I see. A little fire in the neighborhood, huh? An accident with the toaster that provides a teachable moment? Or maybe torch the community rec center just to show who's boss?"

"Not really sure," Constance said, becoming concerned this wouldn't just be a pack-of-gum-style impulse buy.

Madge's eye-rolling was palpable. "Let's just go."

Phillipe was NOT going to lose this sale. "We have a wide assortment, all the way from class A – paper and other solids to class F for that nasty kitchen grease fire. You want to burn metals? Class D for dyno-mite is your answer. Ever seen titanium burn? I have. It's amazing!"

As he spoke, the mentioned flammables stepped onto the showroom floor from who-knows-where, took a bow, and burst into the relevant flame. Constance jumped back every time. Phillipe gestured theatrically and Madge stood her ground, generally unimpressed.

"Fascinating," Constance gushed. "Can you give us a price range?"

Phillipe beamed. "My friends, you are in so much luck right now. Today only, FIreworld is having a…wait for it… FIRE SALE! Everything must go."

"No way," Madge sneered sarcastically.

"Yes, way," Philippe said ignoring the tone.

"How much for something, oh, kitchen sized?" Constance said.

"Ah…doing a little cooking, eh? Class C propane fire is your jam. Maybe the boss invites Fredo over for some cannoli and takes him down?"

"Uh," Constance said.

"That's from a movie," Madge said impatiently. "And not how Fredo died. Can we move this along please?"

"We mustn't be hasty," Phillipe said to Madge. "Fire is..alive. For everyone it is a different experience. The heat and speed and power. It is both friend and foe; helper and destroyer. The right fire for your life is not a choice to be made quickly."

"You're so right," Constance gushed.

"My friend," Phillipe said, putting a gentle arm around Constance's shoulder, "come. Let me show you some options." He escorted Constance to a patchwork quilt of flame that hung on a far wall of the showroom. Each patch burned from orange to blue to white hot, radiating its own kind of hot. Some even burned cold.

Madge shook her head. She couldn't help but think of the time she and Constance went shopping for a simple stomach virus and returned to central office with an army of locusts and a robot tank battalion.

"Don't go crazy over there, Constance," Madge called.

"Please," Constance said. "I'm just looking."

The next week, Phillipe was named sales-creature-of-the-month. He got the good parking spot and was allowed to live at least another thirty days.

For procuring the infinite supply of hilarious trick birthday candles that never burn out, Constance was made head of purchasing. For attempting to extinguish them with the blood ocean Madge insisted on picking up on the way back to central office, thereby staining the calico-patterned carpet in the central office rumpus room, Madge was demoted to an eon of wetting her fingers and trying to extinguish the unextinguishable candles.

Remember kids: fire good, blood oceans bad. And never the twain shall meet.

Inspired by Atari's SWORDQUEST: FIREWORLD from ATARI BYTES episode 215. Stories good. Fire bad.

FATE'S FATE

Carter, the regional fate manager sat back in his office chair; the good, leather one with the armrests and the lumbar support he had to wait to get until after the director of coincidences retired and that guy was damn near immortal. He cupped a brandy in his weary hands.

This had been a good day.

"They really liked it, didn't they?" Carter asked after taking a sip. He turned to Yasmine, assistant to the regional fate manager. Yasmine looked weary. In truth, she always looked worried. That could be because members of her family kept turning up in Hell with little or no due process to explain the reassignment. That wasn't fate's department, so Carter was a little fuzzy on the details. Hell assignments came only from either upstairs directly, from Death Division, or occasionally from the Bad Choices complex. Carter, though, dealt only in fate. And today had been a fatefully good day.

Yasmine looked up from her phone. "Yes, sir. They seemed to like experience quite a bit." Behind one ear, Yasmine had a ballpoint pen; behind the other, a stylus for her phone. Both glinted in the overhead lighting. It was a bit annoying.

"'Quite a bit'?" Carter parroted. "They liked it 'quite a bit'?" He chuckled. "No, Yasmine. They goddamned loved it."

Yasmine winced and waited. Nothing happened.

Fate devoured an entire key lime pie that just appeared out of nowhere, then said. "Those two, what were their names?"

"Joel and Cordelia," Yasmine said, while frowning at her phone.

"Right," Carter said. "Remember how cool that adventure was? They thought they were just going out for avocado toast for the bosses at their internship. Then fate – that's me – intervened and they wound up with diamonds and a chase through Central Park."

"Which was weird since they live and interned in Salt Lake City," Yasmine pointed out.

"I know, right?" Carter the Fate beamed. "And

that bit about going over Niagara Falls in a rain barrel was insane, wasn't it???"

"Indeed," Yasmine said.

"I mean, they loved it right? A mariachi band and ninjas AND feral pigs all showed up. It was the adventure of a lifetime," Carter said. "Can't top that. They'll talk about that adventure the rest of their lives."

Yasmine scrolled a bit on her phone, frowning some more. "Yeah, only, here's the thing."

"What?"

"Well," Yasmine said reluctantly. "It seems Cordelia and Joel want…another adventure."

"Another adventure?" Carter said, bewildered. "They just finished the last one. They've still got buckets of pixie stick powder in their nether parts."

"Nonetheless," Yasmine said, "bio-scans indicate they are jonesing for more adventure. They are so high on the adrenalin rush, they need more. In the course of an afternoon they also went from total strangers with a mild antipathy toward each other to being super horny. Hours of post-adventure sex hasn't quelled it. It might be the pixie powder. You need to give them another adventure."

"OH COME ON!" Carter groaned. He banged his fists on the table, paused, then shrugged. "I can't. There's nothing more to give. Fate deems their lives to be predictable from now on."

Carter made a show of finality by shuffling some papers on his desk.

"So that's your final word?" Yasmine said.

"No. This is," Carter said. "Cumulonimbus."

With that, Carter turned away from Yasmine and stared at a Magic 8 ball on his shelf.

Yasmine, the assistant to the regional fate, got an idea… "Well, that's fine, sir," she said. "If you don't think you have what it takes."

"Well…" Carter said slowly.

"I mean, what right does fate have to hand two ordinary people another extraordinary adventure," Yasmine said. "It just isn't done, is it?"

Carter shook his head. It would be unusual. Fate couldn't deliver all the time. You know, unless you're a one-percenter. Or a Kardashian.

But then, to Carter's great confusion, Yasmine started to recite a poem.

Your life is a bore (Your life is a bore)

We totally get you (We totally get you)

Where the fun comes again for her and him,

It's Adventure II

Surf down to the Earth's core (Surf down to the Earth's core)

Run with gazelles too (Run with gazelles too)

We've got adventures to put smiles on every face

It's Adventure II

The good life will call again, YOLO is totally true…

Down at our dragon zoo (down at our dragon zoo)

It's Adventure II

Yasmine finished and blinked at Carter for an awkwardly long time. "Why did you…?" Carter started to ask, then let it go. Yasmine's words, odd as they were, stirred something inside the regional fate manager he hadn't felt for a long time, not since steering those Titanic builders toward the glory of innovation in ocean travel… though admittedly that hadn't worked out quite as planned.

Carter tossed back the rest of his brandy and a bonus shot to boot. "Right," he said. "Let's do this."

Yasmine was proud of having motivated her boss, but also a little trepidatious. The bottle of brandy on the credenza did not go to waste.

Within days, college stoners Joel and Cordelia were off on a second adventure of a lifetime. They climbed mountains. Outran avalanches. There was a car chase through Italian marketplaces. Cordelia won a camel race. Joel punched an alien from another dimension in the face – or at least the area where a face probably was.

It was epic, in the least cliché sense of the word. Carter really outdid himself as fate conjured adventure after adventure. He was a sweaty, exhausted mess, sure to get that promotion to fate director for the southern dimension. Yasmine had never been prouder of her boss.

Joel and Cordelia grinned the whole time, even the terrifying parts. There was no question this was a day – just one day, but still! – they would remember for the rest of their lives.

…which turned out to be about six hours. Because that's when city bus number 4 mowed them down.

Carter did NOT get the promotion.

But Yasmine did.

Inspired by ATARI BYTES episode 216, where we played ADVENTURE II. Still fun, even if you never played Adventure I.

BAXTER VERSUS THE MERMAID

Probably because he'd been sitting in the sun all day in jeans and a blazer, pounding kombucha and lattes instead of water, Aaron Baxter was getting a bit light-headed and his mind was drifting.

"I kind of wish she'd put on a shirt," Baxter thought. "And yet, not really."

"She" was, well, her name was unpronounceable to humans, but a rough translation is "She Who Delivers Peace and Tranquility to Rival the Quiet Ocean on a Moonlit Night". Aaron Baxter, though, had taken to calling her Jessica. He knew not why.

"Jessica" was a mermaid of the classic wooden figurehead on the bow of a ship variety, though very much real; her human torso flowed into the tail of a fish. Her long silky hair flowed majestically as she swam and her skin was smooth and glowing. Baxter marveled at this. He himself tried every cream known to man to subdue his crow's feet, yet Jessica's face was flawless despite the constant barrage of sun and water. How does she do it?

Baxter was drifting again.

"Fifty-one percent," Jessica said, rocketing to the surface and gliding onto a rock. "Not a percentage point less."

"But…" Baxter said, called back to the moment, "but that would give you a controlling share."

"You want this deal done," Jessica said. "That's what it'll cost you."

Did we mention Jessica the mermaid was a killer business negotiator?

Baxter, on behalf of his company Baxter Development Corp, was pursuing the company's latest "aqua-venture". It was to be the single largest ocean-front development of its kind. He liked to think of it as the thousand-mile Great Wall of China of development deals, but not in China and with less walls, but with more shopping districts.

"Well, can we do business?" Jessica said.

"I'm not giving you fifty-one percent of this aqua-venture. That's insane. Why would I make a deal like that?"

Jessica smirked. "You know why."

"No. I don't."

But, truth was, Baxter did know. Well, the little boy within him did…

It was thirty-six years ago. Baxter was nine. He wasn't the highly successful businessman he is now. He was just a punky kid. One of his buddies was turning ten and threw a pool party in a nearby town.

Jessica the mermaid was also an unknown, fish-American, yet to make her first million. She was working as an entertainer at children's parties; swimming and diving and singing the occasional song. Seemingly ageless, she looked much as she does today.

One night after a gig, Jessica won a small jackpot on some pull tabs that she wisely, if unwittingly, invested in some fish-futures, then a friend's scuba diving business. Jessica got smarter and craftier with her business ventures. Some boat rental services. Some ocean front property. Then – thanks to the most recent presidential administration – she started buying up parcels of the ocean itself. It's complicated how that happened, but her motives were pure.

But Baxter's buddy's birthday party was before all that. Back then, Jessica was a struggling up-and-swimmer who needed work. Krill ain't cheap. Jessica would sometimes pick up octopus garden rent money working children's birthday parties. She'd splash around, do some dives, maybe spray some parents with water. The kids loved it.

Little Aaron Baxter was a guest at a lot of these parties. Aaron was the kid you always see running too fast around the edge of the pool, throwing buckets of water on the girls, hogging the ball during water volleyball. That kid.

Baxter was also the kid who wouldn't shut up when the performer was doing her thing.

At one point in her show, as the kids crowded around the pool, engrossed, Jessica said, "All right, everybody, you're in for a big surprise," as she prepared to do the big show-stopper.

"No," Baxter said. "You're in for a big surprise."
All these years later, the words rattled around in
his head as he examined them. "I mean, URINE
for a big surprise." He laughed the laugh of the
humorless.

Then little Aaron Baxter leaned over the side of
the pool and peed into it.

Now, here's the thing. That act under any circum-
stance is uncool. Problem is, it's especially prob-
lematic for mermaids. Generations ago, mermaid
scientists discovered that mermaids are allergic to
urine of any kind. It almost wiped the population
out, 'cause when you gotta go, you gotta go. King
Neptune decreed that henceforth mermaids would
expel their waste in other ways – like podcasting.

Although she was blistered and achy for several
days, Jessica survived the boy's piss-sault. But
she never forgot it, nor did she forgive. She asked
around and found out Aaron Baxter's name and
burned it into her memory, just waiting for the
day she could whip it out and get him back for
whipping IT out in her pool that day.

And now that day had come.

Like that giant drum of cola that tastes so good going down, then all at once floods your bladder, the memory of what little Aaron did that day came home to company CEO Aaron all at once.

He might have peed a little again. Accidentally this time. He gave in on the deal.

The new development – helmed by Jessica – flourished, though in a completely environmentally friendly way. The ocean actually came out cleaner from the changes.

And Aaron? Well, Jessica is thinking about getting him a new broom.

Inspired by the game AQUAVENTURE from ATARI BYTES episode 217. Who doesn't love a mermaid?

BAD POETRY CORNER: ODE TO ASTEROIDS DELUXE

The grinding out of game sequels

Not even old games are immune

Some are quickly forgotten.
But for others on your shelf make room.

Oh, there's Adventure II
And Pitfall II is like I with flare.
Many follow ups don't suck,
But can any one of these compare
To the mighty Asteroids Deluxe?

What made Asteroids Prime so genius
Is fully on display.
Still multi-directional asteroid shooting.
But maybe it's harder to play?

Don't even try to hyperspace
That's one strategy that just won't fly.
But here you can put up some shields,
So no need to wail and cry.

Two side fins and a narrower body.
This ship is smokin' hot.
All those asteroids and saucers

This ship gives them all she's got.

Don't understand the gushing?

Know nothing about Deluxe?

You'll have to take my word for it.

This game is worth the bucks.

Inspired by ASTEROIDS DELUXE from episode 218 of ATARI BYTES. This is one of the few times the story, or poem, from the show relates directly to the game in the episode. I must not have been feeling well that day.

MOON'S WEEPER

You have to admire the tenacity of crickets. They don't care what happens. All they care about is chirping for a mate.

The crickets on Silber IV, first planet in the Brunton system, are particularly hardy. The two, blood-red moons in the sky above are powerful orbs of celestial power. Still, the crickets are always there, totally not intimidated. Sun rises. Chirp. Sun sets. Chirp some more. Whether the moons shine high in the sky or whether it's total darkness; it's all the same to the crickets of Silber IV.

The chirping, though, was starting to bug the little girl Gar who sat in the tall grass outside her village. The panicking, too, was sort of irritating. This was a good time to panic, though. Gar was sure of that.

She had, you see, just killed the moon. Both moons, actually.

Not on purpose, of course. Gar wouldn't kill anything on purpose. But all day, the village's storyteller had been promising ghost stories after dark. The storyteller was tall and well-mannered, but with a booming voice that would wake the dead – fitting for this event, it seemed to Gar – and he had demanded two things: that the children stay absolutely silent during story time and that it be absolutely dark.

As the sun set that night, Gar could hear the other kids of the village running, laughing. Clearly, the story teller's first request would be a challenge. At least, she hoped, the setting would be right; absolutely dark as the storyteller commanded.

"Be gone, moons," Gar shouted to the sky. "I banish you." No moon would mean total darkness, perfect for ghost stories. Gar need only sit and wait. She laughed. But as she watched the sun slip into the deep pool of twilight, only a velvety black poured in.

No moons.

The girl stared desperately up at all the empty overhead, becoming increasingly worried. She wanted to hear the stories, but she didn't really think the moons would go away. She couldn't really kill them, could she? Worried, she skipped the stories and went home.

The next night, Gar's older brother Aster sat cross-legged on the floor of the family dwelling trying to reassemble a particularly greasy Carbonix from memory. The squealing was already making him crabby. It didn't help that Gar was constantly stepping over the Carbonix to get to the window, jostling Aster's hand, causing him to mis-apply the epoxy.

"Come look, Aster," Gar said. "Do you see it?" Gar's face was pressed against the glass, peering into the moonless sky.

"Shut up, doofus," Aster said. "I'm busy."

Gar lay in bed that night, pondering the enormity of the vast moons slipping away. She'd learned about the phases of the moons in school. Full moons. Half moons. New moons and all that. Could this be some sort of astronomical trickery?

Another night passed. As the sun dipped low, tinting the partly cloudy sky lavender, Gar began to panic. What if there's no moon up there again tonight?

Before long, darkness spread over the colony like Aster's epoxy spread over the floor when Gar kicked the bottle the night before. The epoxy was silver. The sky was black. Totally black.

No moons.

Gar screamed. "Not again! I'm so sorry, moons, I didn't mean it." Her moons-weeping was deep and trembling. It was heartbreaking.

Except to her brother Aster. Aster was not im-pressed.

"It's cloudy out," Aster said. "You can't see the moon because of the clouds."

"Oh," Gar said, hopeful, but not convinced.

By day four, Gar was a wreck. She skipped school to sit on a hill overlooking the colony. The hill put her that much closer to the sky, as if being closer to the heavens would reveal the moons of Silber IV were just messing around, hiding just out of sight in some sort of cosmic joke on Gar.

"Please," Gar pleaded. "Come back. I didn't mean it."

But yet again, once the sun made its final wave goodbye, the sky was moonless. The stars twinkled, almost mocking the moon murderer.

Though tears did roll, Gar was no longer sad. She was furious. "Moons!" she screamed. It was useless, of course. The sky remained empty. "Well, so be it," Gar muttered, resigned to the way of things.

And that's when Gar used the power of her mind to blow up the planet, returning unharmed to the nether realm of the gods.

Don't F with Gar, folks.

Inspired by MOONSWEEPER, in ATARI BYTES episode 219. I dunno, maybe I was grumpy.

THE UNDERSEAN

King Neptune sulked upon his mighty throne of coral; encrusted with the shells of all manor of exotic creatures from the unseen depths of the ocean floor. The king tried to go full-on sulk, but the water's natural buoyance kept sweeping him forward, ruining the effect he was going for.

The doors to the throne room parted. Neptune saw his subjects, the sea life beyond, drifting by. The squid. The blowfish. The weird, deep-water sharks with the extraneous heads no one on land ever actually sees. Daily life washed over them as peacefully as water passing over fish gills.

Neptune wished he felt as peaceful.

His wife, the queen Salacia, floated into the throne room as the doors closed behind her. She sparkled like the glow of bioluminescent algae. "My darling," she said with the faintest ripple on the water.

"My queen," Neptune said, flat like a hammerhead's, well, head.

"The god of the sea should be a bit more cheerful, my dear," Salacia said.

"A king cannot be expected to be cheerful all the time," Neptune said defensively.

"What about Old King Cole?" Salacia pointed out.

"He's got those fiddlers three," Neptune pointed out. "Who wouldn't be cheerful?"

Salacia got a faraway look in her ocean blue eyes. "He has that really big pipe too…"

"What was that?" Neptune said.

"Never mind," Salacia said. "So what troubles you?"

Neptune sighed; a miniature tsunami roiled the room. Finally, he said, "Most of this world is water. By rights, our kind, the sea life, should rule all. But the humans, they ignore us. They overheat our waters with their machinery and cause the sun to burn down hotter upon us. They devour our crabs and lobsters, hunt our whales and frighten our brothers and sisters with their submarines."

"Yes," Salacia agreed, for it was true.

"And despite all of that," Neptune said. "The land dwellers really don't know us. They know the gods of war, of the underworld, of the lands above. But they don't know me. They don't remember my power. They don't…they don't…" Neptune searched for a word, or had it, but didn't want to use it.

Salacia, though, was fine with it. "They don't fear you," she said for him.

Neptune nodded. "All the great kings. They all have a thing. A thing the humans remember about them. Midas turns everything he touches to gold."

"King Henry killed all his wives," Salacia said. "That's a thing people remember I guess." Her eyes went dark. "Don't even think about it."

"Of course not, my love."

"Aragorn ruled Middle Earth," Salacia said.

"See!" Neptune, suddenly animated, said. "More people remember the Middle Earth of old than remember the seas of our domain!"

"Maybe that's a bad example."

King Neptune was on the verge of achieving sulk. "Stupid fiction."

"Do you like turkey legs?" Salacia said. "In paintings, kings are often holding turkey legs."

Neptune shook his head. "I seek a symbol of power, not gluttony."

Salacia, a placid river as she glided smoothly across the throne room, considered this for a while. Finally, she said, "A sword. You need a mighty sword with which you can slay your enemies."

Neptune twirled his beard a bit. "I dunno. That's kind of medieval-y."

"A cannon," Salacia said. "No! A tank. The humans will surely take note of you gliding forth in a tank."

"Perhaps…" Neptune said, but he didn't sound convinced.

Days passed. Salacia went about her business daydreaming about King Cole's pipe and being the goddess of salt water. Many heated arguments were had with her team as to whether humans could be allowed to drink it or not. "Screw them," Salacia said. "Let them drink fermented grain." Little did she know what that comment would unleash upon the world.

One morning, eyes on fire in a way not seen since the oceans parted, Neptune burst into Salacia's bath in the midst of her daily ablutions. With a wild laugh, he whipped out his trident. "Behold," he bellowed.

"Magnificent," Salacia said, dropping her sponge.

Magnificent it was. The three-pronged spear was forged from the iron of the gods. The trident was encrusted with the finest jewels of every color and light danced off of them in a dazzling display.

Neptune held the trident high above his head. The crown, the beard, the wise decision to stop wearing crocs. And now the trident. This was the look of a mighty king, nay, a might god of the world's waters. The humans would have to pay attention to the seas now.

A few days later as Neptune sat upon his throne, clutching his trident, Salacia slid into the room, looking unusually taciturn.

"What troubles you, my love?" Neptune bellowed with vigor and confidence. His trident waggled most godly. "Has the word spread that mighty Neptune has raised his trident in anger at their dismissiveness toward the fearsome oceans?"

"I, well, I don't know how to tell you this," Salacia said.

"You can tell me anything, my dear," Neptune said. "Though, perhaps, you should not have told me that thing about Jupiter and Saturn on the mountaintop. I'm still a little nauseous."

"It's...difficult..." Salacia said.

Neptune straightened his crown, sat tall upon his throne and gazed adoringly upon his trident. "Fear not. If they show the proper respect, I shall try always to be merciful with the humans."

"Well, Tuney," as Salacia often called King Neptune affectionately. "The thing is, the humans have a brand of gum called 'Trident'. So that's what they think of when they hear 'Trident', not you and your...mighty...weapon."

The king blinked a few times. The trident clattered to the floor, echoing across the cavernous throne room.

"Oh. Goddammit."

Salacia's eyes narrowed. "As you wish."

And that's when seafood allergies were invented.

Inspired by ATARI BYTES episode 221: FATHOM.
The sea is a cruel mistress…

JACOB'S OTHER LADDER

The round of applause rose up to meet Jacob as he
descended the towering ladder to the sky. He felt
a wild temptation to fall back and body surf across
the goodwill and admiration of the assembled
crowd of onlookers and potential customers. Jacob
grasped the ladder's rungs and squinted up into
the sun as the breeze wafted through his luxurious
beard. The warm glow of the heavens from which
he descended carried him gently back to Earth.
This was a glorious day.

How did he get this lucky?

The Ladder Emporium was the east coast's premiere purveyor of ladders and height-reaching
mechanisms; or so Jacob said in the locally-pro-
duced, monotone ads he recorded for local TV and
radio, to air between the ads for car dealerships

and podiatrists.

The ladder business was good – top of the world, he'd tell people. Not great, but good. All that changed one day; the day he stepped up to the next level.

That day, Jacob started a build on what seemed like a typical oak ladder, destined to be the ladder in some college professor's home library. Jacob was good at this. He made all kinds of ladders: decorative ladders, utilitarian ladders, even ladders for Dilly Doggone Dolly's saloon playset, in which, despite boasting fifteen points of articulation, Dolly's little plastic arms were unable to reach the little plastic sarsaparilla bottles on the top shelf behind the bar. Jacob, therefore, had come up with a custom-Dolly sized solution so that her customers – like Sheriff Feather Body and Cowboy Clam - would stay hydrated. It was a big hit at local flea markets.

Jacob was just about to insert the last pocket hole screw in the professor's ladder when he had a thought. This ladder was an excellent build. The finish on the wood was perfect. The rungs spaced just so. It was beautiful.

So beautiful, Jacob thought, why stop here? So, he kept going. Rung after rung. Foot after foot. The ladder grew in proportion to Jacob's determination that whatever quest he was on now was even bigger than this ladder itself.

The ladder extended out of the workshop, through the showroom – of course the Emporium had a show room – out into the small, well-manicured patch of grass in front of the shop.

He stood the ladder up. The top reached high up on that one tree he loved in the front of the shop, the one he liked to imagine had lived for a century watching life come and go, come and go. Being able to look down upon the mighty, aged elm tree from atop this ladder he created was both inspiring and awkward. He was almost embarrassed for the tree in its inferiority.

How, exactly, Jacob was able to build the ladder even as he climbed up it, he didn't know. But build it he did. Higher and higher, into the clouds. Were the clouds always so low or was he now so very high? Jacob didn't know, just as he didn't know where the wood and screws were coming from and why they were always at hand. All he knew was that he had to keep going.

As he climbed and built, built and climbed, the heavens opened up. A triumphant anthem swelled as Jacob was welcomed into another realm where light and shadow were one and all knowledge was before him. It was so peaceful there. In the distance, souls traversed time and space itself to call to him, beckoning him to share the love they offered.

Jacob was never a religious man; never really much considered the afterlife. He didn't know if this was HEAVEN or something else. But one thing was certain:

His customers would pay huge for a ladder that went this high.

And they did. Soon, the skies were full of ladders. And those ladders were full of joyful laughing people. He didn't know what the people did up there and he didn't care. Remarkably, no one fell. Some of them cried and a few of them barfed from altitude sickness. But they still came.

For a while.

For the day came when Jacob stood on the top floor of the skyscraper that now housed The Imperial Ladder Emporium smoothing the lapels of his finely-tailored suit and looking through floor-to-ceiling windows to the horizon before him. He was struck by a shocking realization.

No one was climbing his ladders.

Where were all the ladder people? He called downstairs to the storefront. There was no line of customers waiting to buy Jacob's heaven ladders. There were no reservations to climb existing ladders. It seemed this glorious fad Jacob had created had just…ended. Fads don't do that, do they? Even if you work really hard on them?

"What will become of me?" Jacob muttered sinking into his imported Italian leather straight-back office chair foot massager and butt tickler.

The elevator that lead to his penthouse office dinged. A woman stepped out wearing a top hat out of which flowed long red hair with orange streaks. Her boots tapped rhythmically across the office floor and she stood before the crestfallen Jacob, rye smile on her face.

"Can I help you?" Jacob said unenthusiastically.

"Aren't you wondering how I was able to stride straight up through the middle of your building and into your office?"

Jacob looked the woman up and down. "You're really tall. Especially with the hat. Everyone who works for me would be scared of you. What difference does it make anyway? I'm ruined."

The woman glanced out the office windows at that decidedly not-busy skyline. "Yes. Things do look grim," she said. "You could be out in the street in days what with no revenue and the huge overhead on running a building like this."

"Thanks for cheering me up," Jacob said.

"BUT," the woman continued. "I represent a… well-known figure with great power who is prepared to offer you a fantastic business opportunity."

Jacob sat up a little straighter.

"My boss has the schematics for a new ladder you may be interested in," the woman said.

"But what…" Jacob said, hesitating. "What ladder

could top a ladder that takes you to the top of the world and beyond?"

"Well," the woman said, perfect teeth flashing. "What goes up, must go down."

"Uh…"

A jagged hole tore reality open between Jacob and the woman. Waves of heat smacked Jabob full in the face as flame licked the painting of Jacob himself that filled the ceiling of Jacob's office.

A great ladder of the darkest onyx rose from the flame like a blooming flower from the devil's own garden.

It was sexy as hell.

No pun intended.

Yes, it was.

Jacob was entranced. Within days, scores of the new Underworld Excursion ladders went on sale.

Customers lined up to descend to the depths of the Earth and perhaps beyond. They were eager to glimpse the nether realm – out of curiosity perhaps or to settle old scores.

"We're saved," Jacob said to the portrait on the ceiling, now featuring two blackened front teeth, singed in the top hat woman's demonstration.

Only, the thing is, Jacob didn't make any money. He actually lost money on onyx, which isn't cheap. And he couldn't recoup his costs because no one paid their bill. Probably because once they descended the ladders, they never came back.

Damn.

Before long, Jacob was out of business. The skyscraper was lost in bankruptcy court and Jacob sat across the street watching his building get plundered by the tax men and creditors.

Broken, Jacob mournfully glanced over at a frustrated young girl playing nearby with a Dilly Doggone Dolly Saloon playset. She couldn't make Dolly's short little arms reach those sarsaparilla bottles. "Darn it," she said, rather more loudly than her mother would have liked.

Jacob perked up, if only a little. "You know," he said. "I think I can help with that."

Inspired by ATARI BYTES episode 222: ATARI CLIMBER. Climbing to new heights of storydom.

A QUEST UNITES THE WORLD

The post is just a shaky, cell phone video. The lighting is horrible. The audio nearly as bad. Most of the screen is taken up with a man in a brew pub baseball cap. He has a three-day beard growth. Good teeth, but he wears a tortured expression.

As if speaking from inside a fishbowl, the man, who is not identified, mournfully cries, "See!" He gestures wildly. "Why no see! I need four you see."

The video ends at that point. At first, it was posted and shared from one social media account to another. The video's origins were obscured. If anyone knew who the man was or where he came from, the knowledge was lost.

Maybe it was the man's wild eyes. Maybe it was

his missing eyebrow. But there was something funny about him.

The comments were along the lines of, "Lookin' good, unibrow." To be fair, the eyebrow was over the one eye and not really a unibrow.

There was speculation about why only one eyebrow. Some sort of chicken frying incident? Boredom combined with a trimmer? A genetic anomaly? What else did he only have one of?

After a while, though, the shares of the video moved from sites like Face Page and Screamer to become a meme. The meme was a particularly anguished screen capture and the caption "Why no see? I need for you see."

People speculated about the odd syntax. Others thought it was charming. Perhaps English was not this man's native language? But it was still fun to drop the meme in when, say, someone would post some rambling whine about the political flashpoint of the day – maybe the pandemic, or economic woes, or whether or not sticks and stones can actually break my bones and if Congress should convene hearings about it.

After a while, though, the "unibrow can't see" meme started drawing its own scrutiny. Who created it? Who was the guy in the video? Is the beer at the pub on his hat any good? Soon the brew pub appropriated the man's likeness for t-shirts. A clear violation of intellectual property laws, but what are you gonna do? You can't fight the Internet.

People isolated in their homes by the pandemic go out on the balconies of their apartments or stand in their driveways. They sing and dance. They applaud health care workers they know and especially the ones they don't know who still risk their lives for them. All are frustrated. Some are flat out sad. Some are sad enough, they pick up the man's anguished cry.

"No see! Why no see!," groups of citizens, respectfully social distancing, started shouting in chorus. "I need you see!"

Whether the chanting increasesd the people's understanding is unclear. Maybe it didn't actually change anything, but perhaps the release of emotion it provided had benefits on its own.

And that man in the brew pub cap?

He lost that Scrabble game.

"Damn," he told his girlfriend Octavia, "if I'd gotten the seven-letter-word score, I'd have beaten your butt."

Octavia smirked. "Really? To do it, you would have to have had four U's and two C's. I really don't think that was going to happen. Also, not sure that would have been a real word."

Brew pub cap pouted a little. "It was a quest."

"A C quest," Octavia asked.

"Precisely."

"You're so weird."

"Weird…or determined?"

"Just weird."

The world outside stumbled along. Inside, Octavia and brew pub cap went to the other room and totally ignored social distancing guidelines. Twice.

Inspired by ATARI BYTES episode 223: SEA-QUEST. As you can see, often the stories from the show have very little to do with the games from the show. Or very little to do with reality.

ESSENTIAL WORK

Burlsmith worked his way up through the ranks of the Space Protection Force in an era of relative peace. Many scoffed at the career choice. "You're wasting your time," they'd say. "Go into something meaningful. Like medicine. Or the arts. Or politics."

But now that the Earth was constantly bombarded by alien incursions, the Space Protection Force was more valuable than ever. But still they scoffed.

"Hey, buddy," people would say sometimes when they spotted the SPF patch on his jacket. "What good is a SPACE protection force here on EARTH, anyway? It's Earth not space ya know.' Then they'd walk off chuckling as if they were the first to come up with that joke.

The Space Protection Force arose decades ago out of the ashes of the Slurgon insurgence. The Slurgon visitors landed their sleek, silver tube-shaped vessels in the San Fernando Valley unannounced one afternoon. Earth was totally unprepared.

 The squat beings with the wide faces seemed benign at first. Until they weren't. The attack was unexpected and brutal.

Eventually, the traditional military, aided by science and black-market alien weaponry, were finally able to defeat the Slurgon forces. Barely

For once, Earth learned its lesson and Space Protection Force soon became a thing.

A great shield was erected. A literal, invisible cocoon around the Earth that still allowed the transfer of heat and light and sanctioned space vehicles, but denied access to all manner of alien life and technology that threatened our planet.

As chief of daily operations, Burlsmith was essentially a bosun, to use an old-timey sea-faring phrase. A bosun is the crew member in charge of the deck, the equipment, the very hull of the ship.

And much like scraping barnacles off a ship's hull, Burlsmith was responsible for making sure no aliens were able to bond with and permeate the Earth's protective shell.

Much of his time was spent in his office, but occasionally Burlsmith would traverse the shell himself. It was peaceful up here. Best of all, he couldn't hear the taunts and the chants.

Humans, it seems have short memories. Years had passed since the Slurgon incursion. Peace had reigned and people were questioning the need for such an expensive and inconvenient shield. Interstellar travel took a good twenty minutes longer what with the extra security in the upper atmosphere.

"The gate swings both ways, doesn't it?" sneered the editorials on the news feeds. "So is the gate meant to keep evil out or keep us in?"

But then, Space Patrol forces started getting troubling reports. The Slurgon were starting to regroup. There were signs the Slurgon kingdom was developing new, deadlier weapons.

But there was little appetite to actually engage the

Slurgon. The home world was far away. The intelligence was sketchy. The Slurgon had been defeated before. They would be again. Yada yada yada.

But when the Slurgon came back, they didn't just bring the laser mortar shells of old – the humans would be ready for those. This time, they had plasma concussion grenades and what came to be ruefully called "shield stunners". Maybe the humans should have predicted this, but they didn't.

The space force was able to keep the shield around the Earth intact, but at tremendous cost. Many of Burlsmith's fellow soldiers perished. The Earth very nearly succumbed this time.

But you wouldn't know it from the human reaction on the ground.

"Yeah, boyeee," shouted drunken dude-bros from the rooftops. The news cameras captured hordes of screaming humans. Parades were organized, one after another, all over the world.

Then the massacres started.

Noisy parades were just fish in blocks-long barrels. It was easy for the Slurgon insurgents to slip in through cracks in the Earth shield and infiltrate the city streets, shopping malls, even hospitals; wherever the most people were and the plasma grenades could do their worst.

The humans were frightened. They didn't see it coming and didn't know when it would come again. The space protection force was suddenly, desperately needed. The humans were finally grateful their neighbors and friends, brothers and sisters in the force were out there protecting them.

"Stay down," the force advised. "Stay low, Keep a watchful eye out. Limit your time outdoors." Slurgon snipers were known to pick off unsuspecting humans as they walked to work, took their kids to school, did their weekly shopping. It was in everyone's best interests to abide by the space force recommendations.

And the humans, so happy to still be alive, listened.

For a while.

But once entrenched, the Slurgons were hard to remove. The space force would get the attacks under control in one region, just to have more attacks spring up in another region.

The death toll rose overall. Some parts of the world, though, were relatively quiet. And they started to chafe at the idea of curfews and security measures at the entrances to their supermarkets, businesses and houses of worship.

"Why should we stay home?" they started to say? "We're no more likely to get shot by a Slurgon than we are to get hit by a bus."

The difference, of course, was that the Slurgons were attracted to crowds because they could pick off more victims. Curfews and low crowd orders made it less likely the snipers were come.

But the humans just became more hostile. "Let us decide if we go out." Humans do dissension well.

Human after human went on social media to declare, "It's my choice where I walk."

Other humans would counter, "But the more of you INDIVIDUALS who make that choice are putting at risk the ones who don't have a choice –

the space force and med techs and that guy who finagles my flin-flange." Finagling the flin-flange is a complicated…intimate… procedure many humans dealt with at this time in history that we need not discuss here.

The debates were heated and passionate. Frustration, fear and worry are a combustible combination that rivals even the strongest Slurgon missile.

Burlsmith tried to stay above it all. Literally.

Patching the holes in the Earth's shield was stressful. And a couple times he'd had to single-handedly disable one-man Slurgon vehicles as they penetrated weak points of the shield. Still, he'd rather be up here than down on the planet's surface with all that craziness.

One morning, the doors of the space elevator slid open and Burlsmith's assistant Jillick rushed into headquarters. "Did you hear?" she said, out of breath. "They're ending the curfews. The interstellar gate is opening."

"I heard," Burlsmith said, his attention more focused on the game on his phone. Who knew they made a game about excavating cat poops in a litter box?

"Well, what are we going to do?" Jillick said, gesturing at the space shield outside their window.

"Find the one shaped like a bonsai tree," Burlsmith said. "Sort of milk chocolate, not dark chocolate in color. It's worth fifty points."

"Um. What?" Jillick said.

"Never mind," Burlsmith said. He set the phone down, frowning a little. "Do?" Then he chuckled. "Do do. That's funny. Timely too." He closed the app on his phone.

"What?" Jillick repeated.

"I just mean, to answer your question," Burlsmith said, "we'll keep doing what we always do. Our jobs."

"But won't that be harder now?" Jillick said.

"Yep."

"Don't care, huh?" Jillick said.

"I care a lot," Burlsmith said. "Just doesn't matter. The job's the job."

Jillick nodded.

Burlsmith held up his phone. "But first, can you tell the difference between cat poop and ferret poop?"

Inspired by ATARI BYTES episode 224: BEAM-RIDER. Also poop.

BAD POETRY CORNER:

A SMATTERING OF CHAMPION-INSPIRED HAIKU

We are champions.

Yes. Truly, Queen told us so.

Freddie, see us now.

Go from chump to champ.

Not all souls can make the trip.

Many act like it.

How 'bout: Cham PEE on?

You got winning urine stream?

No shake winner's hand.

Champagne starts with champ.

And pain can be part of both.

Drink to the small wins.

The championship

Medals. Trophies. Ribbons. Sure.

I just want fine cheese.

Fruit. Granola. Kale.

The breakfast of champions?

Or lies by posers?

You should be the best

Win! Win! Win! Or, hey, you know,

Just be a good soul.

Inspired by ATARI BYTES episode 225: Championship Soccer. Yes, really.

COMBAT, COMBAT, EVERYWHERE

"Once more unto the breach," General Doug bellowed to his soldiers. He couldn't actually see them, what with the oversized chartreuse helmet. Chartreuse was probably an odd choice for a soldier. He'd have to remember that next time.

"Huh?" came the assembled response from the phalanx assembled behind him.

"Just, you know," Doug said. "Attack them again."

"It's just that…" one tentative voice said. It might have been Doug's major domo Gwendolyn. Or Colonel Connie. Or maybe seventies TV's "Wonder Woman" Lynda Carter.

"Yes," Doug moaned. "What is it?"

"Attacking them didn't really work last time,"

probably-not-Lynda-Carter said. "What makes you think it will work this time?"

"We have to try," General Doug said. "This time, we'll try the hard bristles. Weapons up!"

The soldiers in unison brandished their four-foot toothbrushes with extra-rubbery toothpick thing on one end. The battle commenced.

Reality dissolves away, like toothpaste swirling down a drain.

Doug squints into the blazing sun. Sweat glides down his cheeks. He is a gladiator in the arena prepared to do combat with…what? Will it be a lion this time? A psychotic killer brandishing a spear? Perhaps a fire-breathing dragon that knows nothing but destruction.

Doug turns, head swiveling, making little circles in the sand. The stout steel gates of the arena are still closed. From which will his foe emerge? And when? What will be Doug's fate? Who will be his executioner?

None. He knows it will be none of them. This new

enemy is something unfamiliar. And all the more terrifying for it.

The crowd roars. Doug can't see them. Doesn't want to, really. Someone roars, "Get 'em, Doug! Slay the monster! Wear his ass like a hat!"

"Thanks, Mom," Doug mutters.

One of the gates creaked, slides open a few inches. Something was coming.

"You can do it, Doug!"

"But…but, I don't know…"

The gate slides open a little more.

Doug raises his…broomstick? Where did that come from?

"You suck, Doug," roars the crowd.

"I'm doing my best," Doug pleads. He drops his

weapon which is now a banjo. Picks it up again.
Now it's a precariously tilting tower of children's
building blocks.

Doug swerves to his left as a subhuman cry erupts
from within the gate behind him. The blocks
fall to the sand, the letters on them spelling out,
"DEATH FOR ALL".

The gate slides open. The beast within emerges.

"No, wait," Doug says.

The scene, like grains of sand through the hour-
glass (Thanks "Days of Our Lives") falls away.

The forest is humid and dark. The canopy of
leaves overhead obscures the sunlight. Tank commander Doug waits atop his machine, ready to
overtake the enemy with thousands of pounds of
steel. For once, he thinks, he's ready to give the
adversary a run for its money.

If only he could find his adversary.

Static crackles in Doug's headset. The division

commander barks into Doug's ear. "What the hell are you waiting for? Attack." Easy for her to say. She's safely out of the line of fire.

"I can't see it," Doug reports.

"What?

"I don't know where…it… is," Doug explains.

"That's ridiculous," the division commander says. "We've mapped this out. Just destroy the thing and go home."

"It's not that easy."

"We've got entire villages cowering in fear. Get this done."

"Commander," Doug says, then pauses as he hears the rustle of leaves. Nope, nothing..

"You're wasting time," the division commander says. "I've got to answer to our superiors."

Doug has kind of had it. A deep thud shakes the trees as he bangs down irritably on the tank hatch with one of those oversized head-whacking mallets from old cartoons. Doug positions the mic on his headset over his mouth for maximum audio. He retorts, "Then you come down here and –"

Doug is interrupted by something suddenly moving very fast in his peripheral vision. He stumbles backward, nearly falling off the tank. A massive boom shatters the oppressive silence as the tank fires, though it falls far short of its target. To be fair, that may be because Doug doesn't really know what the target is. Shrapnel falls like so much glittery confetti. Animated cartoon palm trees clasp leafy hands over their ears against the noise.

A dancing monkey - probably a white-bellied spider monkey for those keeping track – is suddenly perched on Doug's shoulder. Dark beady eyes burrow into Doug's. Hot monkey breath warms his cheeks.

"May I help you?" Doug says.

"You missed," the monkey says.

"I know," Doug says.

"Again," says the monkey, wearing a stern face.

"It's hard," Doug says

The monkey laughs. "You suck, dude,"

The alarm on Doug's phone chimes. It's a marching band melody chosen more for the jarring effect of the tuba than out of any love for marching band music. Doug groans and sits up in bed. The dream fades away slowly, but deliberately; the monkey's tiny eyes linger to the end. Was that a wink just before it popped out of reality?

As Doug's senses come back online, he realizes where he is and what his day entails. Just enough time for some toast and a shower. Then off to the lab.

COVID-19 isn't going to cure itself.

A cartoon menagerie of smiling germs lines up along the driveway to wave goodbye as he drives away.

Inspired by ATARI BYTES episode 226: COMBAT TWO. That's not two Combats. That's the sequel Combat, one of the original nine Atari titles. Now you've learned some Atari history. Amaze your friends!

THE COMMUTANTS

The air around Klement swirls and warps. The room he's in is sucked down into nothingness and explodes into the four corners of the universe before settling back into place on Fourteenth Street, across from the bodega.

This isn't new, actually. What is new is this time, though, he thought saw something there with him just as all of reality hiccupped.

No. He didn't just think he saw something..

Really what happened is matter of a new kind had appeared there in front of Klement.

Matter in the form of Professor Noswell.

And it, uh, he, was still here.

"How was your trip?" Klement asks the professor, a standard greeting he supposed.

"Exhausting," the professor says. "Didn't think I'd ever get here." The standard reply.

They both laugh at their hilarity.

Professor Noswell nods to Klement. "Student," he says. "You are on time. Well done."

"We're all on time, Professor," Klement says. "For we never go anywhere."

"That's what separates us from the lesser species," the professor says.

"Well, that and not needing to poop," Klement says. They laugh again.

Klement nods to the other students in the class, though they aren't really here in the room with the professor and him. They are with the professor and themselves – for Professor Noswell is no place, one place and every place. All at once.

Professor Itinerantur Noswell is a noted archaeologist and historian. He specializes in ancient modes of transport, particularly the penchant of early humans to constantly move from one place to another and how they did so.

"As we discussed last session," Professor Noswell begins. "A couple of decades into the twenty-first century, humans began to see the futility of going places and started simply staying home."

"What caused that, Professor?" asks Lill, a student in New East Australia. A three-dimensional representation of Lill flickers into Klement's vision as she speaks. "Did they run out of horses?"

The other students laugh.

"Don't be silly," Klement says. "The early-to-mid-twenty-first was the era of matter teleportation, right, Professor?"

"Well," the professor says. "The historical record –"

"I read there was a pandemic of some sort back then," Brastus, a non-corporeal being from Boston says. "The black plague or syphilis or whatever?"

"So that IS why they stopped traveling," Lill says. "Their horses got sick."

"They still had viruses in the twenty-first?" Milna the cyborg asks. "It's a wonder humans survived unmodified." Her head shakes slowly with a pneumatic whirr.

"Ah, but survive they did," Professor Noswell says. "Beginning in the time of the pandemic, oh, 2050 or so, and throughout the centuries, the humans began to embrace the joys of isolation and solitude."

"What were the humans like before the shift?" Klement asks.

Lill cuts in, quick with a response. "Savages." They often gathered under vast domes called arenas to cheer each other on as they knocked each other down trying to steal projectiles from one other. Very odd."

"Covetous of others' property," Bastus adds. "Shoes mostly."

"They liked to go to meeting places to consume something called margaritas and then… body-surf…whatever that is," Milna says, pointing to a page in a text just out of frame. "Just something I read in the text of an old book unearthed at one of the ancient library excavations."

"Yes, the humans had much maturing to do," Professor Noswell says. "But the point is, our ancestors bore down, sat down and did what needed to be done. Specifically, they got as far away from each other as possible."

"Was this the great purging of ingress and egress?" Klement asks.

"Coupled with the banning of human contact, yes," the professor explains.

"And were they…were they okay with this?" Klement asks.

"Why wouldn't they be?" Bastus says. "Physical

interaction? Touching each other? Ugh."

There is a collective fluttering of the students' avatars as they process the horrifying concept of interpersonal contact.

"I know, I know," Professor Noswell says. "It seems repellant to us, but the humans back then did have some problems with letting it go. They were particularly reluctant to give up…" The professor pauses here, unsure how much his students could handle. "They were reluctant to give up procreative interaction."

"They called it sex, right?" Lilla says. "Because they didn't have mandatory laboratory species regeneration?"

"Quite right. Also, they enjoyed the activity as… recreation."

There's a collective gasp from the class.

"Ignorant cave dwellers," Bastus mutters.

"Did all these social changes work?" Milna asks.

"We're still here, aren't we?" Lill counters.

"Society is judged by its ability to evolve," Professor Noswell says. "By that metric, I think you can say human society has become quite evolved indeed."

"Our aloneness has made us a more unified culture," Lilla says. "Right?"

Klement's mind pushes forth a question that has been lurking for some time. Klement doesn't know how or if he should ask it. The thing about being alone together is even though you're with others, you're separate. Perhaps not being face-to-face (a one-thousand credit fine) emboldens you. So, he asks, "Do any of you ever…get lonely?"

"What's that?" Milna says, sitting up, intrigued. "'Lonely'?"

Bastus smirks. "He means being sad about being alone. As if such foolishness were possible."

"Hold on," Professor Noswell says. "Let's explore this. Explain, Klement."

Klement is regretting his decision. "Well, I just mean…I have these dreams sometimes where instead of ordering sustenance on the vid, I walk through the marketplace and hand-pick my food. It seems…nice."

"Repellant," Bastus says.

"Why would you touch food that others have touched?" Lill said.

"I dunno…just a dream," Klement said.

"Touching food before you buy it," Milna says, "would just open the floodgates. What would be next? Reintroducing scents into our society?"

The world had long since learned to funnel distracting odors harmlessly into outer space.

The professor checks the time. Class is over. Time to vacate this virtual space. Otherwise, this class would meet up with the Study of Limited Movement Seminar coming in next.

Concluding social interactions can be awkward, so society dispensed with it long ago. The class is over and simply ends with everyone abruptly disconnecting.

Klement looks around his living space, bathed in the omnipresent silence. He has nothing to do now but simply be here. Silence and inactivity regain the place they claimed long ago.

And then, as he did every night, Klement glances furtively about the room to see if anyone is watching. Of course, no one is.

He goes to the closet that isn't really a closet and opens the door.

The glorious scents of wildflowers and lavender waft forth from the greenhouse. Tomato plants and apple trees stand at attention. It cost a lot of credits to get Marn to create this hidden room and deliver this stuff to him, but it was worth it. Come to think of it, darkness has settled over the compound; Marn will be here soon for dessert.

Time to put the coffee on.

Inspired by ATARI BYTES episode 227: COSMIC COMMUTER, with credit where credit is due to the enforced isolation of 2020.

STUCK

One early morning as the sun glowed orange and red upon the waters of the cove, a serpent sat sunning himself on a rock. The serpent was gold with red flecks, much like the sun, but its eyes were hard and cold; more so against the life-giving rays coming from above.

Many days, the serpent was a fearsome creature consumed by anger. Today, he was in a good mood. This was somehow more scary.

"Hey, you, pirates," the serpent called. "Remember when you thought you were so clever, making those rude gestures as you tried to sail away and leave me here to rot? Now look at you. You suck at steering a ship. Why don't you give me your vessel? I'll show you how it's done."

"He makes me so mad, he does," grunted Scraggly Beard the pirate, standing at the ship's bow.

The pirate captain and his crew had run aground on this small island and quickly found themselves in a standoff with the serpent. The serpent had been left here by his kind for reasons unknown. Since none of them could leave, they decided the logical thing would be to fight instead.

Scraggly Beard rattled his saber. "I'll lop off his head, I will."

Scraggly Beard's first mate One-Eye looked up from oiling his peg leg and said, "Why, Cap'n? What good will it do? He's just spoutin' stuff. Can't hurt us."

"Yoo hoo, pirates," the serpent called. "Plunder any good treasure lately? Oh, that's right. You're stuck here."

Although a rope ladder already dangled from the deck down to the beach below, Scraggly Beard clenched his sword between his teeth and grabbed a rope hanging from the yard arm, preparing to swing out and land on top of the serpent. He'd seen that in a not yet invented movie once. Once on the beach, he would disembowel the serpent, singing sea shanties all the while.

But then, party pooper One-Eye spoke up. "Seafood allergy," he said.

"Arr, what be you speaking then, good sir?" Scraggly Beard grunted.

One-Eye sighed. Why couldn't Scraggly Beard talk like a normal person. "You get rather…enthusiastic….when you disembowel things, sir. There is a good chance some bits of serpent will get on your skin and with your compulsive licking habit, you could end up swallowing some. That might trigger your seafood allergy, sir. And epinephrine hasn't been invented, as it happens, sir."

"Curses!" Scraggly Beard said. He knew last week's "F-IT, Let's Have a Clambake" event had been a bad idea.

Scraggly Beard waved a clenched fist at the serpent. "It seems we be at an impasse, sir."

The serpent rolled his eyes. "Not really. I'm quite content. Though you bore me."

Scraggly Beard looked at One-Eye as he gestured

with the sword. "You sure we don't have enough epinephrine, matey?"

"'fraid not."

"You know," the serpent called. "If you really want me to go. Just give me your ship. I might even be willing to leave you the peg leg oil. I'll be taking the gold, of course."

"One Eye, seriously…" Scraggly Beard pleaded.

"Well, sir," One Eye said. "You could," he gestured starboard. "..you know. Play to your strengths."

Scraggly Beard didn't get it at first.

One Eye made a V with his arms, then a swooping gesture, grinning so all his gold teeth glinted in the sun.

Scraggly Beard got it. "Say, serpent," he called.

The serpent rolled over lazily on his rock. "You

finally ready to admit you need me?"

"The only thing I need," Scraggly Beard said. "Is to cut off your stinking head and use it as a planter for those pansies One Eye gave me." He turned to his first mate. "They are quite lovely."

One Eye grinned sheepishly.

"But…" Scraggly Beard reluctantly lowered his sword. "Seeing as we are both stuck here and may be for some time, I propose instead a more symbolic test of supremacy, don't you know."

"What have you in mind?" the serpent said, mildly curious.

"A diving contest," Scraggly Beard said.

The serpent was now intrigued. Serpents were sea creatures, naturally, but mostly they just lounged on rocks or below the surface in coves waiting to startle fishermen and the occasional banjo playing frog. It was a rare day, indeed, that they got to show off their fabulous high-diving skills.

The serpent was quickly escorted to the deck of the pirate ship. At Scraggly Beard's order, One Eye half-heartedly waved a sword in the serpent's direction as the serpent slithered over the bow onto the deck, but mostly he spun the hilt around his finger.

The serpent and the pirate slipped into their ever-within-reach speedo bathing suits. As it was his ship, Scraggly Beard insisted on going first. He stepped onto the plank over the starboard side and executed a perfect forward dive with one and a half somersaults in the pike position.

"I've seen better," the serpent grunted.

"Right," One Eye said, gesturing with the sword. "Off you go."

"With pleasure," the serpent said. "When I get back, I'm eating you first."

One Eye shrugged. "They all say that."

The serpent also stepped to the starboard side and did a flawless back dive with three and a half somersaults in the tuck position.

One Eye let out a huge sigh. "Well, that's that."

The starboard side was the one that ran aground on the beach. Well, beach and a seemingly bottomless crevasse. Bottomless-enough anyway.

Whoops. Funny how CAPTAIN One Eye had forgotten that…

Inspired by ATARI BYTES episode 228 SWORDS & SERPENTS for the Intellivision. Swords AND serpents. What more do you need?

BAD POETRY CORNER:

SPACE BATTLE

Things. Possessions. Stuff.

You could put it there.

You could put it here.

You could put it anywhere.

Space is infinite.

Your stuff is not.

Though sometimes it seems like it.

Clothes. Books. Games.

Non-stick pans. Obelisks. And the occasional para-
keet.

How do we accumulate all this?

Where should everything go?

We need space for stuff.
So, we claim it.
Sometimes peacefully.
Sometimes, it's a battle.

What's ours is ours.
What's yours is yours.
Sometimes that's not the end of the story.

Thus, the old joke:

What's mine is mine.
And what's yours is also mine.

The battle is real.

George Carlin said: "Their stuff is shit. And your
shit is stuff."

We love our stuff.

Though now, with recent events,

Maybe less so than before.

And we value the spaces we call our own.

But pandemic has forced us to spend more time in
those spaces.

Ensconced in there, surrounded by stuff, at first
we are cozy

Shielded from the outside.

After a while, though, even much of our own stuff
becomes tiresome.

Old, faded, cheap or otherwise unsatisfying.

Collapsing in on us as we tumble through turmoil,

Like a leaping stuntman's cardboard boxes.

Does the stuff that completes our spaces really
complete our selves?

Maybe the space battle isn't so much about space

As it is about where we fit into that space.

When finally we can go to new spaces,

Will we think about the stuff that can fill it,

Or the selves who can fill it?

Inspired by ATARI BYTES episode 229: SPACE BATTLE for INTELLIVISION and the way even our favorite spaces sometimes shrunk to intolerable dimensions in 2020.

WHAT HAPPENS IN VEGAS ISN'T GOING TO CLEAN ITSELF

When Gene got the call that Las Vegas was re-opening after the pandemic quarantine, he had three demands before agreeing to spearhead the mission to sanitize the place.

First, under no circumstances would a blacklight be used. He'd shined a blacklight in Vegas once. It was….well, he'd slept with regular lights on for weeks after. The weird thing was, he'd been using the blacklight inside an air conditioning duct. Covid-19 would be scared to hang out here.

Second, no one on his crew was allowed to reference Sinatra, Dean Martin, Sammy Davis Jr. or any other Rat Pack related components.

Third, NO DRAMA. Everyone loves to romanticize Vegas. The lights. The glitz. The quick fortunes and quicker bankruptcies. The violent past and gaudy present. There was nothing romantic about Vegas as far as Gene was concerned. Less flowers, more penicillin.

Still, a job's a job.

When the call ended, Gene pushed up his rose-tinted glasses. Why rose-tinted? Gene was a professional sanitizer. There was nothing rosy in his day-to-day, so he had to find the rosy where he could. If only his glasses were rose-scented…

*****

Gene lead a small caravan of trucks into the desolate city. Tumbleweeds scattered like, well, like tumbleweeds. A marque touting "Danny the Magic Man" had all but disappeared behind the dense overgrowth of foliage. Cheap buffet cuts of prime rib, eyeing their chance for freedom, had made it as far as the strip before being devoured by the escaped tigers from the various animal acts around town. Feral sex workers scattered for cover as the caravan rolled through town.

Gene brought the caravan to a halt in front of the "Sand in Your Pants" casino.

While the sanitation team prepped their equipment outside, Gene stepped into the casino. The overhead lights were out, but the glow from the row upon row of unstoppable slot machines was enough to see around the room.

Gene stepped to one of the tables and absently spun a roulette wheel as he considered his strategy. Then he wished he hadn't. Who knew what germs were on that thing?

A tower of poker chips slid off a blackjack table and Gene jumped, in spite of himself. "Great," he muttered. "Now I have to clean that up too."

"Nah, let it be," a high-pitched voice said from the darkened end of the gaming floor. "I gave up on cleaning a long time ago. Really frees a guy up."

Gene peed a little. Good thing they brought the extra-absorbent sponges.

"Who's there?" Gene said, not nearly as bravely as he would have preferred.

One time on a sanitation assignment at a fast food

restaurant that had been shut down by the health department for, quote, "odiferous curly fries", Gene pulled a wad of gunk out of his shop vac that was opaque, gelatinous and, yes, odiferous.

What oozed up in front of him in that casino today, was like that fast food gunk. Only seven feet tall. And it vibrated. Wide, heavy-lidded eyes peered out from an area of the ooze blob a bit lower than Gene would have expected the face to be. Who was he to judge?

The creature's thin-lipped mouth opened and Gene immediately wished it would close again. The stench made the smell of those fries positively morning coffee glorious.

"Hello," the blob said enthusiastically.

"I come in peace," Gene said. "I mean, 'hi'. What are you?"

The creature oozed back on its would-be haunch-es. "That was rude."

"Sorry," Gene said. "Haven't been around people much lately. It's not a pandemic thing. I just don't like them."

"I miss people," the creature said.

"Still hungry are you?" Gene said. "I think I see the croupier doing the backstroke around your midsection."

The creature was alarmed. "No! That would violate social distancing."

"Yeah, we're not doing that so much anymore."

"Really?" the creature said. Gene could swear it shrunk a few inches. He knew what was happening now and, therefore he proclaimed:

"I know what you are."

The creature's eyes grew wide. "You do?" It shrank a few more inches.

"Of course," Gene said. "I go to all these houses. Businesses. The occasional destitute unicorn flophouse. I've seen you before. You're Sid the Id."

The creature beamed. It wasn't pretty. "Party on, dude!"

"The world has been locked up at home for so long," Gene. "No going out to movies. No socializing. No, uh…intimate encounters. All that need for gratification is palpable. It's real, even if we can't see it. It's like oxygen. Or the fascination with cat videos on social media."

"That cat in the shoebox with the remote control is hilarious," the creature said.

"All that desire for gratification, for pleasure, when it's repressed, turns sour. Ugly. Turns into, well, you."

"…Thank you?"

"But you're free," Gene said. "The quarantine is over. People can go out and have fun again."

"Yay!"

"Yeah, bud. All I have to do is vacuum you up

with my shop vac and dump you in a metal drum for disposal in a landfill. Now hold still…"

The creature shimmied like lime gelatin day at a dynamite convention. "I'm scared," it said.

"Don't be," Gene said. "I got a new vac. Nice long hose. Great torque."

"No, not that," the creature said. "I'm scared to go out again."

"Why? People can gamble. Have fun. Get together again. Normal stuff."

The creature sighed. "Normal isn't normal anymore. I don't know how."

Gene laughed. "I'm a guy who cleans up microscopic poop traces off people's stoves and you're a blob made of people's feelings. Normal has never really existed anyway."

The creature thought about this. With a wet, slurping sound, two twig-like arms emerged from the blob's shoulder area and reached out for a dealing shoe off the blackjack table. "Draw," he said. "High card wins."

Long story short, the Sand in Your Pants casino was rendered spotless and stayed that way until Bernard LeTreck won the jackpot on a $1 slot the following Tuesday.

Sid the Id is headlining eight shows a week in the big room at the casino.

Gene gave up the sanitation racket. He manages Sid now. And tries really hard not to touch anything.

Be safe out there, everybody.

Inspired by ATARI BYTES episode 230: LAS VEGAS POKER & BLACKJACK for INTELLIVISION. And curly fries.

QUARANTINE'S MONSTER:

A BAD POETRY CORNER HAIKU OFF

They sit, the man and the woman, looking at their phones. A pandemic has been declared. What's that? Oh, here it is. The woman scrolls briefly through the more or less unbiased, if sparse, news article. She summarizes for the man, who is borderline disinterested. They are clean, well pressed, enjoying expensive coffee beverages in a crowded marketplace. Their bags overflow with stuff they don't really need and mostly barely want. They went out and got it because they can go out and get it. The man tugs at a tangle of chestnut hair. "Really need a haircut," he mutters, speaking over her a bit, not looking up from his phone.

The woman coughs. She's been meaning to make an appointment with the doctor. Probably just a cold. Seasonal allergies maybe.

Across the food court, between the mango vendor and the booth hawking press-on fingernails, the woman sees a very familiar couple. This couple glares at the woman so intently, the woman jabs her boyfriend. "Hey," she says. "They're staring at us."

"Huh?" the man says, glancing up finally. "Hey, dude," he says. "They look like us."

The couple at that faraway table do, in fact, look like Brent and Colleen, the names of our heroes from the before times. The man at the other table, though, has a patchy growth of beard, hair down to his shoulders, and a slight tremor in his hand as he raises a pint to Brent and Colleen. The woman who looks like Colleen seems to have applied her makeup with a trowel, still failing to cover the circles under her eyes. Both people are pale and awkward looking. Their clothes are wrinkled and probably smell.

Colleen breaks her gaze finally. "Weird," she says, and goes back to reading about the pandemic.

Then the haikuing starts. As it does.

Colleen is confident, upbeat.

Probably not bad.

So, a few sick, then better

Still, I have a job.

At that faraway table, mirror dimension Colleen
and Brent smirk.

Man, you don't know we're

Screwed seven ways 'till Sunday

Innocence will kill

Brent takes a huge bite of blueberry scone, gestures to something on his phone and shows Colleen. For the moment, they are willfully taking
little notice of future-them.

This thing will give time.

Paint! Build! Craft! Add a rec room.

Feathering our nest.

Alternate Brent stands and starts to take off his
pants to show their pre-pandemic selves his sol-
dering mishap, but alternate Colleen puts a three-
fingered, restraining hand on what's left of Brent's
knee.

Online drill orders

Discount coded death boxes.

Three-eighths drill bit stress

Brent asks Colleen about stopping at the fudge shop. "How can you think about fudge right now?" Colleen asks, perturbed by their other selves finally.

"I like fudge," Brent pouts. Then he brightens up as another strategy takes shape. "You know…we promised the kids."

"Well, they could use a treat, I guess," Colleen says. "I mean since we won't let them out of the house for a week or so while this pandemic blows over."

Family time is here

Home school. Board games. Sing-a-longs

Online swim classes.

Alternate Colleen's eye twitch betrays her. Alternate Brent pees a bit when a group of kids run by.

Family time. Land mines.

Don't look. Don't say. Live to fight

Another day. Duck!

Suddenly, Brent is seized by an intense round of Googling. Finally, he shows his phone to Colleen who nods enthusiastically.

Sourdough starter.

Learn French. Wrap self in plastic.

Weave a teal throw rug.

Alternate Brent and Colleen pop an antacid cocktail with a Pepto and vermouth chaser.

Have a pastry brick.

Who knew pie, cake, rolls, and bread

Had such low flash points?

Ollie, Brent and Colleen's half lab/half Irish Wolfhound/half schnauzer/half chimpanzee lopes up to Colleen for a gluten free tofu squirrel brain treat. The pets will love all the extra pandemic time with their humans.

Yay! They're my humans!

Skritches, Fetches. Nonstop fun!

Throw the ball again!.

A growl from under alternate Brent and Colleen's table chills what's left of their souls.

Did you hear that? God…

I think he's awakened. Shhh.

Why does he hate us?

Colleen leans over and pats Brent on the arm. "You know," she says. "More home time could mean more…you know…time."

"Online model ship building time?"

Did it. Every room.

Chandelier held us. Yee-ha!

Pandemic kink fest.

Alternate Brent reaches for the non-dairy creamer and brushes alternate Colleen's arm by accident. She recoils in revulsion.

Bad breath held captive

Seriously, whole house, dude.

Pants off dance off? Ugh.

"Well, anyway," Brent says. "I'm fortunate to be a fortune telling forensic accountant songwriter. I can do that from anywhere."

"And I'm a belly dancing, sous chef chemistry book editor. What else are webcams for?" Colleen agrees.

Pajamas at work

Only good snacks in break room.

Relaxed…Productive!

Alternate Brent is distracted, filling out his unemployment application. Alternate Colleen is screaming obscenities into her phone at their Internet provider.

They fired my ass.

Out of work sight, out of mind.

Well, who needs money?

The smiles on the determined faces of Brent and Colleen falter just a bit. They exchange a look.

Maybe this pandemic thing won't be such a non-walk in a non-park.

Unite against foe.

And the world comes together.

We will be as one.

Alternate Colleen and Brent guffaw at this. A green-toothed smile cracking their stoic features for the first time today.

Seriously? Us?

World can't agree on squat. Even

Toddler whines about masks.

Brent and Colleen let this sink in. They drain their coffee cups, stand and go over to the alternate Brent and Colleen's table. They sit and the four of them, not social-distancing, fight the virus with round after round of tequila shooters.

Inspired by ATARI BYTES episode 231: BEAUTY & THE BEAST for INTELLIVISION. There may be beauty in all things, but that pandemic was just a beast.

BEAT DOWN IN PRIME TIME

When you hold a smile in place for too long, smile fatigue sets in. The lips, jaw and eyes become droopy. It's not a good look any time. It's especially not good on camera.

"Allison Eats It All" was MunchTV's tentpole show. Allison Devonay Dubois had been hosting the show for four years. She could cook anything, whether it wanted to be cooked or not. The "blue suede shoes" episode was a staple in holiday episode marathons.

Allison was a brilliant chef and an engaging show host. Her need for perfectionism rivaled the need of cream to clot at just the precise temperature during cool down.

Taping of the latest episode of "Allison Eats it All" was winding down. "I'll tell you what," Allison said to Camera One, "This here dingo dilly is delish." She held up a platter of something fried. Most of Allison's viewers wouldn't know what dingo dilly is. Even fewer would go look for it in the frozen foods section. But ratings for this episode would be through the roof. Why? Because Allison did something that only the best MunchTV hosts could do: make the viewer believe for an hour or so that they care about food that isn't served by number and wrapped in waxed paper.

Allison took a huge bite of dingo dilly, her sparkling eyes and bulging cheeks convinced the camera she enjoyed it. Then Allison spit the dilly into a bucket after the director yelled, "Cut!"

Allison walked off the set, nearly slipping in a puddle of broth evidently spilled from a pot on boil for the next show recording here, "Steven Sucks it Up".

Backstage, Ben Benben was waiting. Ben Benben was always waiting backstage. Ben hosted no fewer than three shows on the network. One of them was a show where he traveled the country visiting bakeries to ask how they make their cannoli and whatnot. Another show had him as host of a competition where well-known bakers compete to see who can make the same cake any of us could make, except theirs looks better 'cause it's on TV.

Ben's third show was his favorite. "Ben Beats It" aired right after Allison's show and featured a different baked treat every week. Ben's cakes and cookies supposedly were SO MUCH BETTER than everyone else's because of how he beat the eggs, which involved no fewer than four implements and an antique diving helmet.

And he was so damn smug about it. Allison hated his ass. Well, she liked his ass. But she hated the rest of him.

Right now, Ben was trying to perfect a recipe for banana pecan scones.

"Beat it somewhere else, Ben," Alison muttered, reaching for her bottle of cook's secret sauce she kept in the "water" bottle backstage.

"But I love waiting in the wings for you, Allison," Ben said.

"Well, you have gotten used to being my second banana."

Ben smirked, holding up his mixing bowl. "Have you ever even seen my banana?"

"Nope. Never will," Allison said, then shuffled off in search of some highly processed food concoction with unpronounceable chemical fillers that enhance flavor.

******

The next taping of "Allison Eats It All" was all about pasta sauces. As she was showing off a hearty marinara, Allison scalded the area between her thumb and index finger on a bit of dripping sauce and realized the pot it had been simmering in was leaking. "Cut," she said, stepping on the director's line. "We gotta swap this crappy crock out."

"Take five everyone," the director said, as if it was his idea.

"Tough break," Ben murmured in faux sincerity backstage. "Get it? Break? Like the pot breaks?"

Allison just made a face and self-medicated from her water bottle.

"So, how are contract negotiations going?" Ben asked.

Allison shrugged. "Same as always. I pull in the sponsors. They always double my salary. Same old same old. Guaranteed five more years with an option for a sixth."

Ben nodded slowly. "Same time slot?"

"Of course. It's the first thing I demand. Well, the first thing, actually, is a steady supply of chocolate liqueur in my dressing room. Then the time slot thing. Gotta go." The pot having been replaced, it was time for Allison to go back to work. She had at least five more years of plastic TV smiles to conjure.

That meant, Ben realized, it was time for him to go back to work too.

******

In the next episode of "Allison Eats It All," she introduced a new segment where she reads the recipe for that week's meal in haiku. This week was all about "one pot wonders", entire meals cooked all in one pot. About six syllables into the recipe for eggplant stew, Allison paused when she heard a sound like…

…well, you know the sound a sheet of ice makes in those "Ice Age" cartoon movies when the ancient squirrel cracks one with an acorn? That's the sound Allison heard from the eggplant stew pot. A small river of stew juice started dribbling out as a crack slid up the side of the pot.

Then she heard it again.

And again.

Okay, it wasn't just the stew pot…

And again. In stereo, it seemed. Ice cracking. Maybe leftovers from that bartending show, "Toast of the Town"?

"Earl," Allision said to her director, quietly as if volume would make the cracking worse, "Earl, what is that?"

Earl shrugged. Earl shrugged a lot, usually with an annoying little squeak. Allison kind of hoped a fjord would open below Earl and swallow him up.

More cracking. It wasn't ice. No, this was something else.

Allison pointed. "There!" she shouted as a crockpot cracked in two on the kitchen island in front of her, sending a stream of alfredo toward the linoleum. "And there," she said. "And there." She pointed a long index finger at pot after pot, seemingly as if pointing a magic wand and making the pots explode. It wasn't ice at all. It was the pots. The pots were cracking. All of them. They were crackpots!

Unfortunately, this show was for soup and sauce week on MunchTV. Every show had some sort of liquid-based food item to feature. Even "Ben Beats It" was doing bread pudding. So the studio was full of boiling liquids in pots.

And now all those pots were cracking, releasing edible napalm into the kitchen set.

Allison nearly died.

Okay, not really. But she did choke on a matzo ball projectile. Earl had to Heimlich her and everything.

The bad news is, this episode of "Allison Eats It" was live. So, the entire dramatic dam-breaking scene was seen by millions of viewers.

Allison was fired from the network the next week. Not because the pots broke, but because, in response to the pots breaking, Allison unleashed a profanity-laced, racist, homophobic, anti-Semitic tirade against, really, anyone she'd ever laid eyes on and a few others she hadn't seen, but just knew they were out there.

"Ben Beats It" got Allison's time slot. This was good because the new contract Ben Benben negotiated came with a hefty raise. He needed the money because it wasn't cheap paying off that night janitor to mess with the thermostat so that the studio got super cold at night. Like dangerously cold. Like maybe even cold enough to crack pottery…

Inspired by ATARI BYTES episode 232: CRACKPOTS and cable cooking shows, which are on TV a lot in my household.

DAN DUNK AND THE DETERMINED DOUGHNUT

"Your coffee's gettin' cold," Dan's breakfast buddy said from across the table.

"I know," Dan shrugged.

"You should just go ahead and drink it," Dan's

breakfast buddy said. "I mean, iced coffee is one thing. A nice, refreshing midday break. But cold, regular coffee? Blech." He laughed a bit at that as bits of icing sprayed out on the blech sound.

"I can't drink it yet," Dan said, shifting a little, causing the upholstery in the booth to squeak and make a little fart noise. Dan's sciatic was giving him fits today.

"Why not?" his buddy said.

"You know why."

"Good for you, man. Business first," Dan's dining companion said. "Don't flake out on me. You're crusty, but you ain't got a flaky crust like some lame ass-cobbler."

Dan snorted. "Pastry jokes. Clever."

A heavy-set man in a backwards ball cap and his fully tatted-up girlfriend walked by Dan's table, looking at apartment listings on the girlfriend's phone.

"Too claustrophobic," the man was saying. "I need

to breathe, man." Out of the corner of his eye, he caught sight of Dan and stopped dead. His girlfriend walked a few more steps before she noticed.

"Dan Dunk," the man said. "You're the dunkman. During the pandemic, when there was no sports to watch and cable ran all those old eating contests? That was you. I watched you all the time, man. You the doughnut king, man."

Dan shifted again. Another upholstery fart. He hoped his fans would understand that. "Thanks."

The man held up his phone. "Cool?" he asked.

Dan grinned awkwardly and sat up a little straighter. The man leaned in for a quick, fully unnatural selfie.

"You goin' to the Phoenix Pastry Push this year, man?" the fan asked as his girlfriend looked increasingly bored. "It's gonna be epic. No way Hollow Gut Dave can beat you."

"I'm retired," Dan said. "Cholesterol and calories, man. They suck. When you're young, your gut snaps back quicker. You get older and..." Dan patted his midsection. "Not so much."

"Oh," the man said, glancing at the custard-filled confection on the table across from Dan. The man's disappointment thudded onto the Formica, rattling the little basket with the sugar packets. "Well, good to see you man. Keep rockin'." The man and his girlfriend shuffled away, scrutinizing a duplex on their phones.

Dan Dunk stared into his cup for a long time, perhaps reading non-existent tea leaves, because this was coffee. Snickering broke the silence.

The doughnut was laughing, weeping bits of icing. "You suck, Dan."

"You're not good for me," Dan muttered.

"What was that?"

"You're not good for me," Dan shouted, startling the other patrons. Baseball Cap looked up, confused…and disappointed. He followed his girlfriend across the restaurant.

The doughnut on Dan's table rolled a half turn to the left. "You weren't always such a wuss."

"I took you out plenty of times."

"So where's the doughnut-eating champion now? Oh, that's right, he's hiding in a diner eating the house salad with dressing on the side."

The salt and pepper shakers toppled as Dan's arm shot across the table, stopping just as the index finger pressed into the doughnut's vanilla icing. A lone chocolate sprinkle fell to the table.

The doughnut grinned. "Do it," it said. "You know you want the crème."

"I've always been more of a jelly man," Dan said. Another upholstery fart.

"Yes," the doughnut said, appraising him. "You have. Soft and wobbly."

Dan grabbed the doughnut in his fist, fingers poised to squeeze the filling out of it. It felt good. Natural. All those years of doughnut eating competitions. Win after win. The money – some anyway, mostly from endorsements, commercials and whatever. The groupies – yes, they exist. All those amazing years on top of his…sport? All those amazing, wasted years.

He was "Dan Dunk". One-two. Down it goes. Bring on the next. Now what did he have to show for it? Borderline diabetes and a second mortgage on his house since he couldn't hold a day job what with all the travelling he did during competition season.

Dan looked down at his empty salad plate – empty except for the hardboiled egg. Why did they always put that stupid egg on the salad? He plopped the doughnut down on the plate, started to lick icing off his fingers, thought better of it, and wiped them on the napkin instead.

"There's more of me out there," the doughnut smirked. "Any good shop will give you a baker's dozen for the right price."

"All done here?" The teenage girl's voice floated into the scene. Dan startled a bit, then glanced up into the face of the smiling, pig-tailed girl wearing a navy blue shirt with the diner's name on it.

"Yes," Dan said. "Yes, I am."

She smiled and took Dan's plates away. Dan had a fleeting image of the smashed doughnut reconstituting itself and leaping from the plate, then crawling into someone else's doughnut box to terrorize them. Or maybe one day he'd buy a box of doughnuts for some kid's charity drive and there that same damn pastry would be all over again, "Twilight Zone" style.

But for now, he was free. He considered ordering a peach smoothie to celebrate.

The man formerly known as Dan Dunk took a deep breath just as his phone chimed. He answered it and uttered the words that locked him on his future course. "Nathan's Hot Dog Eating Contest? Hot damn. Count me in." He went to find Baseball Cap and Tat Girl so they could record a "live" video announcing Dan's return to competitive eating.

The doughnut quivered with delight in the trash bin, oozing happy jelly.

The "Twilight Zone"- esque episode-closing-moral presented by a guy in a dark suit didn't occur here. That dude spilled a generous scoop of minestrone onto his tie and was currently in the restroom trying to get something other than brown sludge to come out of the faucet.

Inspired by ATARI BYTES episode 233: DOUBLE DUNK. And doughnuts. I like doughnuts, as an amateur only.

VACCINE VALENTINE

The hand-lettered banner misspelled "Vaccine", but the sentiment was there. In bold, purple letters, the sign read simply: "YAY, VACINE!" (PRONOUNCE VAY-KEEN)

The newsreader looking out over the crowd assembled on the plaza outside HumanControl Corp, shook her head at the misspelling, and leaned into the microphone. "After months and months of illness and worry, it's fair to say much of the world is relieved that HumanControl Corp. has announced a new vaccine."

One of the newscast's producers coughed up a kidney. Then he cued the next segment before passing out.

The newsreader plowed ahead. "Yes, many will be very relieved. But is this vaccine too little, too late? Joining us now is Dr. Lola Lassiter, head of the federal Division of Science People Are Suspicious Of. Dr. Lassiter, welcome to Actionable News. So, is this vaccine a magic bullet?"

Dr. Lassiter chuckled as she set down her Mai tai. "A magic bullet? My goodness, no. We already invented the magic bullet to hide the evidence after a political assassination. It's lead, not a vaccine." The doctor suddenly realized what she had said. "Oh…." She furtively glanced over at the shadowy figure in the dark suit chain-smoking in the corner. He shook his head and slipped away into shadows even murkier than his own.

The newscaster had to lean back, the wireless mic picking up the squeak of her chair, so that she could look Dr. Lassiter in the face as they talked. The doctor was now hiding behind the chair. "But, Dr. Lassiter, has your division signed off on this HumanControl Corp's new vaccine?

"Of course. We sign off on everything they do," the doctor said. "No questions asked."

As a graphic appeared on screen showing the

monolithic HumanControl Corp HQ high atop a hill and angry villagers approaching it from below with pitchforks, the newscaster said, "Some people have criticized the company's vaccine, haven't they?"

"Have they?" the doctor asked, as she made the dust bunnies behind the set look a bit more like actual tiny little bunnies. "How so?"

"You suck," a man shouted as he walked through the studio. "Vaccines are the tool of the oppressor." Then he fell on his face as he tripped over the coffee cart because he was staring at his phone instead of where he was going. Also, his face fell off. The coffee maker toppled off the cart and cracked when it hit the floor. The entire production crew wept.

"Look," Doctor Lassiter said, "Take bunnies like this one." She held up one of her dust bunny creations. "Only, you know, with blood and organs and stuff. The company tested our vaccine on, like, a bazillion of these things. Most of them died horribly, but then we did the same thing with, like, fourteen whole humans who needed the cash. And they were fine. So far."

"What about the worries that vaccines are inherently unsafe. That they have unintended, dangerous side effects?" the newscaster said. "How can you be sure the vaccine is safe?" The newscaster's newsreader monotone rippled just a bit into emotion territory.

Dr. Lassiter stood finally, brushed the dust, old chewing gum and a prophylactic wrapper from behind the set off her pants and looked the newscaster in the eye. "Look," she said, "I'm not a politician. I wasn't hired as a spy or a secret agent or some sort of…of…mad scientist type. I can't even grow a good scraggly beard. But I get it. Vaccines are scary. HumanControl Corp.? Big time scary. The federal government? Slightly clownish at times. But the world is a mess right now. People are sick and dying. I have a cousin who looks like a frog now because of all this – wait, that's from something else. Not all bad. Flies are cheaper than gourmet cheeseburgers. Anyway, what was a saying?"

The newscaster evenly course-corrected. "You were commenting on the efficacy of the vaccine," she said.

"Right." The doctor nodded. "Sitting around watching it happen isn't an option. The time is now. I would never sign off on this vaccine if I didn't believe it was safe and necessary."

The newscaster put a finger to her earpiece as if that would help her hear better, but mostly just looked like a thing news people on TV do. She looked to the camera and said, "I'm being told the crowd has moved out from the plaza and reassembled along the side of the road. We are told that the first batch of vaccine is being delivered this morning to the plaza from a production facility across the country. Delivering such a valuable product over the open road is a dangerous proposition these days, of course, what with the roving bandits, hijackers and a scarcity of beef jerky in convenience stores. Although we would expect that the vaccine might at least be arriving in some sort of armored truck, we're told actually it will arrive just moments from now in a car the company describes as, quote, 'that car from 'Knight Rider' coming down from a cocaine bender'."

Dr. Lassister pulled a hood over her head and put on dark glasses as she bolted from the TV studio .

The newscaster pressed her earpiece again. "I'm being told a vehicle is approaching over the horizon. This could be the first delivery of the life-saving vaccine that will usher in a new age of hope and health."

The crowd roared as engines could be heard in the distance. It started low and unsure, but as the vehicle approached, the noise crescendoed. The vehicle dodged dino-copters, mercury landmines, other things that go boom. An irradiated, zombie gorilla crapped on the vehicle's windshield. Yet it kept on rolling.

The cheering was deafening as the vehicle rolled to a stop in front of HumanControl Corp. The driver hopped out and delivered… a ZombieZone package to Becky Carruthers in purchasing, who simply loves the value pack radiation gloves ZombieZone offers. They even come with a code for a free MP3 of high-pitched squealing that will keep the mutants away at night.

Surrounded by a wall of cameras, Becky ripped open the package and a couple dozen packets of gas station condoms spilled out. The driver laughed, slipped his shades back into place and drove off in his '85 Toyota Tercel. With the money he could make for this vaccine on the black market, that driver would be able to buy two Tercels.

Meanwhile, somewhere near Cincinnati, the sleek, low to the ground, perfectly free of mutant slime, all glass interior, electric car of the future commissioned by HumanCorp was parked by the side of the road. It's driver, Brent, was trying desperately to change the flat tire before hill people came down, stole his car and restocked the convenience stores with human jerky.

Brent had just gotten the second lug nut back on the wheel when hot breath on his neck told him he might not get to the third one…

Inspired by ATARI BYTES episode 234: FATAL RUN. Get your shots, people.

POND-CAST

The audio sting finished and the host leaned into the microphone. "You're listening to the Frog Pond-cast! Proud part of the Drain the Swamp Network!"

Darrell "Frog" Pendergast, 34, hit pause on the recording as he queued up the voicemail for the next segment of the show. He hit "resume".

"Now folks," Frog said, not sure he wanted to go down this road, but unable to stop himself, "you know we've been doing the Pondcast for a lot of years. In that time, well, we've made a few enemies. Back in the day, the Pondcast had a co-host. Turtle Bay Tuttle was my boy. We grew up together, college-ed together. We were best men at each other's weddings and sat in the front row for each other's divorce trials. We were inseparable….until we weren't."

Frog sighed. "The swamp is a dirty place, friends. And Turtle Bay? He's a dirty, dirty…reptile? Amphibian? Whatever. Point is, it's the old song, the old…hey, won't you play another somebody done me wrong song. And that somebody was Turtle Bay Tuttle. Now, I'm not gonna rehash all that now. I been over all that in past episodes. You long time listeners will remember the famous… on-famous?…in-famous? Episode where Turtle walked out on us. Go back and listen if you want. 299 I think. I coulda pulled it from the list, but you know my rule about lookin' stuff up.

"Anyway, I got no secrets from you people. So, today, I got a voicemail from Turtle. I was totally blown away. After all that crap went down, I pulled his number from my phone, wiped it from my memory even. But he still has mine I guess. I'm telling you this because, well, the no secrets thing. Also, he left the voicemail on the pond-cast phone line. So…it's fair game for the show. I'ma gonna play it for you. For a little extra fun, I haven't even listened to it yet."

Frog hit pause, coughed, took a sip of grapefruit seltzer, belched, sipped again, and restarted the recording. "Here we go."

Frog hit pause, belched again, restarted and pulled up the voicemail. Here's what the Pond-cast audience heard in a gravelly voice:

Leap away, you turd.

You sit all day, croak away.

Suck down flies, turd boy.

Frog turned off the voicemail. So, it was true. Frog really was the bigger man. No way would he leave an immature voicemail like that.

The waveforms on the recording software flattened. Silence ate up the seconds. Nope, no way would Frog ever stoop to childish jabs.

Well, maybe just one.

Frog leaned into the microphone. "Okay, everybody. That was…I mean, I know Turtle and I didn't separate on the best of terms, but come one. It's like…it's like…

Hey, Turtle Tuttle.

A hare could kick tortoise ass.

You big dumb dummy.

This was not Frog's finest work. Haiku was tricky. He rushed through the end parts of the show where he talks about social media and where to email him and saved the recording. Once edited, he posted the thing and tried to focus on a hard reboot for the next episode. Until…

A few days later, Frog opened the next episode of his podcast this way: "He's back, friends. The turtle's head has emerged from his ass, I mean shell, and he dropped this little tuttle turd on the ol' voicemail."

Warty McWartWart

Your tongue is long, sticks way out.

Most of you does not.

Frog ran right up to that line just before you lose your stuff, looked out over the edge into the black void where the anger and bile bubbles in a hot mess of stuff you shouldn't say, but surely will. The cool breeze of rationality still ruffled his hair, but he ignored it, of course. He said:

Go to hell, half shell.

Turtle, tortoise, terrapin.

Turtle Bay fails life.

Late that night, one final voicemail from Turtle Tuttle came in. Frog listened to it a bunch of times, sitting there in the dark. He almost didn't play it on the next episode. But, you know, no secrets, right?

Tortoise beats the hare.

When frogs barf, stomach hangs out.

Frog not worth my time.

How dare Turtle bring up the stomach thing again. Frog had SAID he was sorry about that. On the next recording, he shot back.

Turtle lives long life.

Empty nothing on half shell

Less than flies to me.

After that, listeners waited patiently for weeks for another episode of Frog Pond that never came. Turtle, meanwhile, started a new show with his buddies Pup Dog and The Fish.

Frog mostly just sat around in the dark.

Inspired by ATARI BYTES episode 235: FROG POND and my beloved podcasting.

BAD POETRY CORNER:

FRONT LINE! CONSTANTLY ON THE FRONT LINE! SO DAMN EXHAUSTING...

*With apologies to The Eagles for no reason whatsoever

He was a raging commie liberal; he thought knew all the answers

And she was a neo-conservative

She pissed him off and he tweeted her letters

As culture wars rained down from above

He had a nasty reputation, lots of attitude

They said she was a conspiracist; prone to self-delude

They had one thing in common: they were both scared of Covid

She'd say only sheep wear masks; he'd say so many dead

Life on the front line

Pandemics or China or Russian espionage

Life on the front line

Politicians love nothing more than the game

We use social media against our enemies to take aim

They hated different people

They honed their sourdough skills

They protested intently

They made their thoughts known for good or for ill

She cheered Operation Legend; his friends were picked up

She pretended not to notice the op was really f-ed up

The world is at war; ripe for the fight

We're all too tired to sort it

We don't get it, but we fake it

Life on the front line

Going out of our way to hate mankind

Life on the front line

Protests and counter protests, desperate to be heard

The reality gets lost

Everyone ready with an angry word

She said, "Listen sheep

You gotta face the facts

The mainstream media makes you pudding
brains.

Just look how people who don't look like me act."

He said, "Racists and anti-vaxxers,

Slow your roll a bit.

People should drive policy, not the anti-taxers."

They were rushing toward an election.

Each begging for their person to win

They didn't care, just tryin' to get shots in.

That's life on the front line.

You could choose to laugh or cry.

Probably both.

That's life on the front line.

So terribly sorry.

Inspired by ATARI BYTES episode 236: FRONT LINE and, you know, life today.

THE COLD SHOULDER

The Ice-o-Lator stood atop the frozen mountain that was once The Stop 'n' Squat Convenience Store. Bennie Benmen was encased in a wall of ice that filled the now useless exit door, trapped mid-bite; his corn dog now more popsicle than cured meat with breading.

Ice-o-Lator laughed a hoarse guffaw, puffs of chilled air ravishing the warm air molecules of this summer night and leaving them breathless. The super villain's icicle teeth glinted in the sunlight.

Inside the store, clerk Mallory tried to carve her way to freedom from her frigid tomb with her nose piercing. Meanwhile, the bitter cold rendered customer Alex Appleby's intended prophylactic purchase unnecessary.

From atop this snowy abomination, the Ice-o-Lator spoke to the frightened citizenry via the cameras on the news choppers circling overhead.

"People of Town City: It is I, the Ice-O-Lator. I have brought your city to its knees. Your urban area is under my control. The metropolis is molded to my will. Your populace is pummeled. Your…"

The villain's villainous rant was cut short as he slid on his butt down the slippery slope of Mt. Squat.

And that's when the Ice-o-Lator awoke from his dream. He irritably switched off the heating pad and sat up with a groan. With a curse as he tripped over his frozen kitty, the Ice-O-Lator went out to the kitchen for a snifter of brandy. The liquid burned as it slid down his throat. Ouch.

The Ice-O-Lator looked around his small, one-bedroom apartment. Giving up the spacious supervillain's lair had made economic sense; who needs all that room when you're constantly traveling the globe spreading evil and ill will?

But now…here he sat. What good is a globe-trotting supervillain in a pandemic? He could no longer spread fear and frosty badness with a mere touch of his finger when collecting change; the simple brush of a cold shoulder in a crowded subway. Social distancing kept him away from everyone, which was kind of okay because people who weren't the Ice-o-Lator sucked.

But icky as people are, you couldn't wreak havoc upon them without actually being among them,. You can't entomb an army in sleet via video conference.

"This pandemic totally frost-bites," the Ice-O-Lator muttered.

The Ice-O-Lator was weeks into the pandemic before he figured out he needed to wear oven mitts when he made his sourdough or else his frozen hands would dry it out.

"Zoom and popsicles" isn't as fun with frozen treats. Going on a computer to watch each other lick popsicles is just…weird.

He tried doing a jigsaw puzzle, but one of the center pieces – the eye of the peregrine falcon, the one in the top hat, not the one in the English style fedora – fell down the heating vent. The last time the Ice-O-Lator touched the heating vent, the collision of cold and hot created an ice storm that was hell on the carpet.

The Ice-O-Lator's Ice-Phone X vibrated across the table. He smirked as he looked at the caller ID. He took the phone's temperature, spritzed it with sanitizer, and hit the button. "What?" he said.

"Lator, do you wish to join me in bringing the American military forces to their knees?" said the Humidor, a humidity-based villain known for spreading unpleasant sweating and wrinkling of garments across the land. "Their camouflage gear doesn't breathe well."

The Ice-o-Lator considered this. It would be nice to get out of the house, but, you know, Covid. Would…would I have to go outside?" For the first time ever, the Ice-O-Lator was…nervous.

"The marines don't yet have drive-thru maneuvers, so, yes, Ice-O-Lator, there will be going outside," the Humidor said. "Though next week, I am going to decimate that world supply of gold. They have curb side service."

"Well, I was planning on a full day of planting fake medical studies on social media," the Ice-O-Lator said. He just couldn't bring himself to walk out that door.

"Oh…," the Humidor said. "Well, bye then."

The call ended.

The Ice-O-Lator sighed and walked to the window to look out on the world. The parking lot was full – nobody was at work after all – and a wide world stretched beyond. So many potential victims for a super villain. But he just didn't have the heart. Nature had beaten him to the punch.

So, the Ice-O-Lator opened the window and sent a blast of cold breath that caused the air to drain from the tires in that parking lot. Whenever his neighbors got ready to go back to work, at least they would be mildly inconvenienced.

Inspired by ATARI BYTES episode 237: FROST BITE. Also, yeah, I don't know what this is, but I do know even supervillains have feelings.

BAD POETRY CORNER:

NUMBERS ARE DUMB

Numbers are dumb; let me count the ways.

Yes, I see the irony there and I don't care.

For too long, numbers have gotten a free ride. They're numbers, price them like it. Make them work!

What's dumb about them, you ask? Here we go…

One is the stupidest number.

Look at it.

It's all like, "I'm number one."

Stuff always comes first to it.

One is arrogant too.

And its cockiness rivals

Even stupid number two.

Because for all one's problems

Number one at least denotes wee.

While our friend number two

Stands for something much more stinky.

Three. Such a clunky number.

You came in third. Third wheel.

The first three digits, a useless trio.

Intense hatred is all I feel.

Four. An even number to be sure.

Even. As in level. As in boring.

Let me lay out all four corners.

Hey, stop that. I hear you snoring.

The only good five is a fifth of gin.

Why group anniversaries and all with hall moni-
tor five?

Five fingers, sure. That's no excuse.

With him around, hard stayin' alive.

Six sounds like sex, but much less fun.

Adds up to only half dozen. So so lame.

Six a.m. much too early.

Six lovers, I won't play your game.

Seven is a liberal hoax.

They scream out, "lucky number." Indeed…

Seventh heaven, they'll tell you, means great joy.

To soft-headed ruin seven leads.

Two-four-six-eight

Who do we appreciate?

Not looking at you, number eight.

Truth hurts. Kidding. Truth is great.

Dressed to the nines

Is a thing people say

To cover the 9 mm ick

Of having nine in your way.

And there's zero. Let's all sneer!

"Oh, our dear zero, heroic nullifier."

But zero is literally a hole

Props self next to one for ten. Liar!

Inspired by ATARI BYTES episode 238: FUN
WITH NUMBERS. Numbers suck, people. Remember it.

USING YOUR HEAD

THUNK

Sir Steinway Pettifogger flinched and glanced up from his leg of lamb. He set down his flagon and rubbed at a point on his head west of the bald spot. His wig maker would be shot at dawn.

Pettifogger was sure he'd felt something strike him upon the top of his head. But no one else was in the room.

The cold ooze of the egg yolk seeped through the curls of Pettifogger's sparse wig and onto his ample cheeks. The confused nobleman wiped irritably while his chamber maid continued her repulsive service. Why he needed to relieve himself in the dining room, she would never understand.

A mysterious, hooded figure wound his way down the back steps, chuckling.

*****

The ladies in the courtyard fanned themselves; a mild defense against the warm breeze and Elizabeth's flatulence problem.

"Can you believe the behavior of that foul Reginald in the salon yesterday?," Ann asked, once she'd regained her wits.

"Despicable," Elizabeth said, wrinkling the other ladies' noses with her foul breath. Some of the ladies wished their husbands would get around to inventing dental hygiene. They were tired of hiding the brushes, floss and whitening strips they had already invented themselves, what with all the misogyny.

Elizabeth continued. "I do believe Reginald is a well-known cheater at backgammon."

"Still," Charlotte said. "It was quite upsetting. My servants spent hours getting the blood stains out of the carpet. My delayed morning tea was a bit tepid."

High atop the courtyard, the stranger crouched on a balcony covered with lilac. He waited for just the right time. Once the ladies' attention was distracted by snickering at a servant having a mishap with a stack of chamber pots, he leaned quickly over the balcony. It was time to strike.

Four fresh turds, the source of which we need not go into, tumbled from the balcony, one for each head. The response was pretty much what you'd expect.

The servant thought it was funny though.

The stranger ducked back down out of sight and skittered back into the manor house. He felt a little bad for the already overworked servant who would have to deal with their outraged charges, but oh well. Such was the price of education.

*****

The royal navy flagship was a sight to behold. Tall and proud, it owned the seven seas, ready to subdue all bounders bounding over the waves.

Also, the yardarm was really high up. A great vantage for the man dressed in the distinctive orange and black plumage of the Scottish Crossbill.

The edible brown crab claws waved in the breeze as they dropped from the "bird's" hand with a practiced flick of the wrist. The admiral never knew what hit him. The ensign who had been forced to swab the deck because his cuffs had only two buttons instead of three, though, saw the crab assault coming and snickered lightly to himself as he applied mop to deck.

The man-sized bird shimmied lightly from the ship's yard and shuffled down the dock. Because it was difficult to see through the beak, the bird ran straight into Edmund Halley's Comets. No, not the celestial body. That's just what this Earth-bound astronomer/geophysicist/physicist body called his fists – the two comets. They don't come around often, but when they do, you remember them.

So the bird struck Halley's comets and flopped to the ground. Halley pulled the mask off the bird man and shook his head. "What's the third law, bitch?" Halley said.

Unmasked Isaac Newton groaned and held his busted nose. "Action and reaction," he said. "When an object exerts a force on another, the other object exerts an equal and opposite force."

Halley kissed both fists. "Yeah, baby." He hoisted Newton, the founder of the famous three laws of motion – every object in a state of motion tends to stay that way; velocity is constant; for every action there is an equal and opposite reaction – to his feet. Newton shoved Halley away then, sort of proving his own theories.

"Why you doin' this, man?" Halley asked. "All the dropping and what not?"

"They don't understand," Newton said. "They don't appreciate the gravity of gravity."

"So, you drop stuff on people's heads?" Halley said.

"Of course," Newton said. "The law of attraction. Objects with mass – like the massive behinds of the privileged class – attract smaller objects. I just thought those coddled, ignorant elites needed a little demonstration."

Halley grinned an evil little grin. "Stickin' it to the man," he said.

The two scientific icons high-fived. "The science way," Newton said.

Then Halley and Newton went and got drunk on this new fad called gin.

Inspired by ATARI BYTES episode 239: GRAVI-TAR. Bitch. And science!

TOPPER CAN'T SPIN

When the toy box lid was closed, as it usually was, Topper was never able to see the outside. He wondered sometimes what went on out there.

He heard things, of course. Kids playing. Dogs barking. The occasional nondescript scream. Some of it was scary and made him happy to be in his isolated little toy universe. But most of the time, he wished he could be free.

And sometimes he was. When the toybox lid was left open and the light from the big bay window shone down, it felt good. Even better was when Topper got to come out and do his thing.

Spinning. Twirling. Gliding down the sidewalk sometimes. Spinning until the tree-filled vista with mighty branches stretched so high above him, toward the sky, became a whirling blur of leaves on sparkling twigs, then was still again as the child's toy came to rest.

Topper lay on the ground, unconscious, for hours afterward. When he awoke, the world had changed. The gyroscopic effect, the certainty of direction that ruled Topper's existence…was gone.

And it scared him.

Bartleby Bear lumbered down the sidewalk toward Topper. Although the favorite toy between Christmas Day and December 27, Bartleby's battery-powered voice box was crackling and had lost its mellifluous tone. His moveable joints worked though. He actually thought Donna, the toys' person, still liked him best. Stupid bear.

"Topper," Bartleby Bear grunted. "What are you doing?"

Topper tried to shove himself into a crabgrass-filled crack in the sidewalk. "Spinning," he whispered. "Just spinning."

"Too bad," Bartleby barked and kicked Topper into a small cluster of rabbit poops in the grass.

Topper tried to shrug off the slight. Things happen, don't they? His buddy Bouncy Ball always said, "You gotta roll with things." So Topper should too. It would be hard – he was a top whose natural inclination was to sit upright after all – but he would try.

Later, as Topper vibrated lemonade glasses while spinning on the picnic table, Stuntman Stew Stunt Cycle did a wheelie between the pitcher and the citronella candle before Stew sailed over the edge of the table, toppling Topper with him.

The starry night scene painted on Topper's upper half came to a stop. "Dang it," Topper moaned. "My stars…" What did he do to deserve this?, Topper wondered.

Nothing, of course. The answer was nothing. Yet, here he was.

Topper spent the next three days in the dark toybox. While he was in there, he overheard Donna talking to her mom. Donna always wore orange from head to toe and got bored easy so conversations never lasted very long.

Her mom said, "Bunny…" Her mom often called Donna "Bunny". Maybe because she couldn't remember Donna's real name? Topper wasn't sure. "Bunny, you need to pick up your toys. Leaving them all over the floor is dangerous. They could get broken. People could trip on them."

"You really think so?" Donna said, clearly distracted. "I'm not sure." She wandered away.

The toys didn't get picked up.

The next day, Topper was out amongst the flowers and patio furniture on the back patio. Spinning. Spinning. It was glorious. The painted stars were a swoosh of yellow and silver as they should be. Topper was certain with a little extra propulsion, he could become airborne.

And then…

Topper nicked the edge of a toy drum and, startled, careened into a minefield of building blocks. He stuttered and skipped over the wooden blocks, the lower half of his vertical axis snapped clean off and he came to a rest in the grass near the sprinkler. The water was cold and relentless and only barely masked Topper's tears.

Donna watched this play out from the other end of the patio, considered it for a moment, then, unconcerned, she hopscotched over the scattered toys before making her way back into the house.

Topper never spun again. Eventually, long after the stars had faded as the sun bleached Topper's paint, Donna's grumpy dad would deposit him in the trash.

The moral of the story, kids: PAY ATTENTION TO WARNINGS AND…PICK UP YOUR DAMN TOYS.

Inspired by ATARI BYTES episode 240: GYRUSS. My kids never learned this lesson. Ever.

PLANET OR WING IT

Welcome to PLANET OR WING IT, the show where we help the newly evolved dominant species on a given planet decide whether that planet is the perfect home for them to ironically exploit after overthrowing the previous dominant species for doing the same thing, OR whether they should conquer and colonize some other planet just 'cause they can….provided the sinks have good back splashes and the bathrooms have been updated.

I'm your host, Lance Lackey! Let's meet our guest!

Doctor Z is the leader of a newly evolved race of talking apes which has taken over Earth. The apes are trying to decide whether to stay on Earth and make this suffering, decimated planet their own cozy bungalow or whether they should overthrow and colonize some other unsuspecting planet.

"Lance, buddy," Doctor Z told me, "We love our smoldering home so much, but we're worried about having space for the kids. Our kids. The human kids can bugger off."

We hear you, Doctor Z. We. Hear. YOU!

Since the nuclear war devastated Earth, the once vibrant and thriving planet has become a bit of a wasteland. Even their most valued works of arts have fallen into disrepair. It would require substantial tender loving care to make it homey and is perhaps the greatest fixer upper in the galaxy at this time. We're not sure a thousand voiceless, conquered humans could put it back together. That's why some of Doctor Z's associate believe that it would be a better use of their weirdly anachronistic weapons to colonize another planet that is move-in ready.

"Also," Doctor Z told us, "it would help if a new planet was cool with cruel, invasive experimentation and occasional lobotomies." He paused, then added, "And if it had hardwood floors."

But that's not all these picky rulers want. "When the humans were in charge, they were able to extract the minerals they needed from the ground, harvest their crops and butcher their own animals," Doctor Z lamented. "Ape-kind is above such menial tasks. "That knowledge died with them in the nuclear holocaust – which they definitely caused, I might add.

"Now that we are in charge, we're seeing just how much work all this is," Zaius told us, gesturing widely. "Listen, I have no doubt conquest was the right call, but I don't know how they humans did it."

The doctor's associate piped up, "Well, you know what they say: human see, human do." He guffawed awkwardly at that, then, more seriously, said, "We could enslave the humans and force them to work for us."

Doctor Z looked nervously at the camera. "Kidding! He's kidding. "

Perhaps he was kidding, but when we suggested

the new ape empire perhaps needed to go somewhere less high maintenance instead, he bristled. "You mean space travel? Like those other…never mind."

We assured him we can find a planet that's an easy commute from the human work farms.

"No conquest required?" Doctor Z asked.

No conquest.

"What would be the point of that?"

Anyway…

Earth is rich in natural resources this fledgling dynasty could take advantage of. Not only are there many empty buildings left standing from the wars. Some of the water is not irradiated and those weird, mute psychics living in the rubble will happily portend future events ominously.

And the chance of occasionally spotting travelers from the past wearing loincloths lends a quirky element you might not get on other, less eclectic planets.

Still, Earth is sort of a been-there-done-that planet now, isn't it? So, we offered Doctor Z some options:

Beeltug XIV is a ways out on the outer rim of the galaxy, but boasts lots of natural light. Being super close to the sun will do that. While the apes would have to ship water in from other planets because the heat has boiled away the Beeltug oceans, the wide-open, craggy vistas and lack of competing life forms on the rocky planet make this peaceful planet attractive indeed.

Fartus, in contrast, is a densely forested planet where the jungles teem with screaming vegetation. But they scream in harmony, so it's quite lovely. At night, though, the planet is quiet – all the better to hide from the spiders – and cozy. A welcome retreat for a conquering force.

But, you know, conquering apes gotta conquer, so maybe the Apes would like a planet that would provide another new fun bit of genocide. The mole people of Surrendus are just waiting to throw down their pointy sticks – gently, though, because if you slam a pointy stick down too forcefully, it could still bounce up and stab somebody - and be taken in by the next invading force. It might as well be the apes!

But when we went to offer a new home to the apes, Doctor Zaius shook his head. "Don't look for it, Lance. You may not like what you find."

The he lobotomized the production crew.

Until next time, this is Lance Lackey leaving you with this thought: Damn you. Damn you all to Hell.

Inspired by ATARI BYTES episode 241: PLANET OF THE APES. Also, cable home buying shows which is what's on at my house if the food channel is in reruns.

BAD POETRY CORNER:

WE DO NEED ANOTHER HERO

So this guy Giovanni Amato,

Up there in early 20th century Maine,

Had a dream to feed the masses.

"We're so hungry," customers complained.

A bit of ham, some provolone.

Veggies and condiments.

Giovanni gave them what they wanted.

But bread was the big draw; paid the rent.

No plain stuff. Italian or French.

One bread short and plump.

The other long and narrow

Gives the sandwich game a bump.

Call it a hoagie, sub or hero.

Pile it high with ingredients.

Kettle chips, slip the pickle.

Put all in your face with expedience.

Why a poem about sandwiches?

Not heroic like soldier, cop or protester .

But when life is mucked up like today,

A good sandwich makes all of it better.

Inspired by ATARI BYTES episode 242: H.E.R.O.
I'm hungry. Be right back.

KING DEMON ATTACKS

A great shriek rumbles up from the bowels of
Hell, signaling the end of the commercial break.

Hunger slaked by the entrails of a more or less
willing production assistant, the host of the daily

program, "Demon Attacks", the King Demon himself, once again assumes humanoid form. He has an unsettling sheen and dark eyes you could fall into and endure an eternity of pain if you looked directly at him.

The Demon King looks at his ad copy and speaks into the microphone. "Today's episode is sponsored in part by the Devil's Food line of snackables. Remember: they're the DEVIL'S food. If you want them, give us your soul…while supplies last."

The Demon King turned his gaze slowly toward his guests, who blanched, but stayed steady.

The Demon King's face displayed a smile of goodwill, assembled from the teeth of his victims. He spoke again into the mic. "My guests today, the Good Witch and the Bad Wolf, are competing for the office of Leader of the Gateway Land. The battle of wills will commence on November 3.

"Before the break, I was asking the candidates if they have any concerns about the subjects – nay voters – entering the Gateway Land to pledge their souls during this time when the great purge is wiping out humanity faster than the humans' own failings could ever hope to?"

The Bad Wolf snarled, great puffs of steam billowing from his nostrils. "The humans will do what humans must. And they will do so with typically timid, human care."

The Good Witch gestured majestically, the shine of her crown – an affectation rather than a sign of nobility - glinted in the Demon King's dark eyes. "Well, we can't live our lives in fear, can we? I live to serve the Gateway Land and that dedication is worth the risk."

The Demon King watched the two candidates for a long beat before his voice rumbled forth again. "Wolf, you stand accused of lying to the damned about the inevitability of their fate. How do you respond?"

That snarl again. "The facts speak for themselves, Demon King," the wolf said.

"And I speak for the facts," interjected the Good Witch brightly.

"Does that not strike you as presumptuous?" the Demon King asked.

"Yes, certainly. Being a good leader means presuming all the time."

The Demon King regarded the Good Witch. "I am not certain you know what 'presumptuous' means."

"Perhaps, but I presume to know the Bad Wolf is bad for the Gateway Land economy."

"Well," the Demon King said, "What – "

"Because he is," the Good Witch interrupted. "Bad for the economy."

"May I speak to that accusation?" The Bad Wolf said.

"I would expect no less," the Demon King invited.

"The Gateway Land economy is complicated. It's fine for the humans to say 'Give us your money and we will give you the services you deserve as we see fit.' But in the Gateway Land, money is useless. Our currency is fear and hopelessness. We need much of both to keep things running. The river of blood won't damn itself. The spider armies can't trample those who would flee without the right equipment. The demons – like your own spawn, Demon King – must feast if they are to go out into the universe to enslave the populace. All of this requires many human souls to be collected. I will do so proudly and with great zeal."

The Bad Wolf wrenched the head from a gargoyle and munched it with great alacrity into the microphone. The Demon King was nonplussed. "Some would argue there are only so many souls to go around. Why should the Gateway Land demand more of them?"

The Good Witch made a face as she daintily put away the last few bites of the still beating heart presented to her by an enthralled supporter just before the supporter spontaneously combusted. She dabbed at the corners of her mouth with the dried skin of a Bad Witch who had long since ceased to be a bother.

"You might as well ask why there should be a Hell at all, mightn't you?" the Good Witch asked. "Look, the existence of humanity depends on the balance of good and evil. I don't like it. You don't like it..."

The Demon King glowered at the Good Witch.

"Okay, maybe you like it," the Good Witch allowed. "But you're powerful and in control. The rest of us, we need to know we have choices; choices between doing what's right and what's expedient, which isn't always the same thing. One or the other is going to serve the purpose at that moment, but we may be so caught up in the moment that we don't see it. The Gateway Land is crucial to making that clear. As leader of the Gateway Land, I will know what's best for you. And, through me, you'll know it too."

"She is a fool," the Bad Wolf grunted. "Only I know what is best for you."

The Demon King leaned into the microphone. "Actually, the ones who know best for us all are our friends at River Styx Shipyard and Consultation. Need to know your fate and how to get there? Let River Styx Shipyard and Consultation be your guide. Free initial consultation. I'd like to thank my guests, the Bad Wolf and Good Witch. Remember to vote on November 3. Your souls have always been on the line, but never so much as today. Trust me. Stay tuned for the Hour of Fear hosted by our friend Reaper. Don't fear the Reaper, just listen from two 'till three."

The Good Witch and the Bad Wolf stared at each other. The studio vibrated and the walls bled.

Queue commercial for foot fungus relief.

Inspired by ATARI BYTES episode 243: DEMON ATTACK. Remember, everyone: vote early and often.

BAD POETRY CORNER:
KNIGHT AND DAY

In the age of old
When evil had free reign.
One brave soul stood up
Fought to restore peace a-gain.

And his name was Pegasus
"Wait for me," calls Lancelot.
But Pegasus has no time.
Too much evil causing good to rot.

"Oh, c'mon," whines Lancelot. "I'm a knight."
Sure, but Pegasus is an equine winged descendant
of gods.
The knight grins stupidly, "My sword is so
broad."
But can he fly over enemy clods?

What do girls love most?
Well, anything they want of course.
But often, that is horses.
Suck on it, Mr. My-Non-Hooves are sore.

What use have I for you, Lancelot?

I'm fast and powerful and strong.

I run like the wind and soar over clouds

You, armored sir, piss your hinges all day long.

It's true sometimes the knight is useful.

He can open doors, tell the king of our deeds.

But if I had opposable thumbs, Sir Lancelot,

Night would fall for the knight, you'd see.

An invasion force amassed on the border.

Come good knight, be quick about it.

I shall ride into battle, you right behind.

Someone must hold my horse crap bucket.

Inspired by ATARI BYTES episode 244: SIR
LANCELOT. Also, I like horseys.

ROB 'N' HOODIE

The front door slammed shut. On the wall, a
framed photo of Einstein riding a unicorn vibrated
and was still.

Rob tossed his keys into the faded Big Bird tray with the crack in it and threw down his backpack with a thud. Forgot the laptop was in there. Whoops.

"Where you at?" Rob called.

The two-bedroom apartment answered with silence.

He tried again. "Come on, we'll be late."

"That's funny," a voice called back. "No one has been LATE for anything for months."

Rob followed the sound of his roommate's voice down the hall and found him in the second bathroom, looking at himself in the mirror. He was making weird expressions.

"What are you doing?" Rob asked.

"You ever look at yourself in the mirror?"

"Sure…" Rob said. "I've tried brushing my teeth not looking in the mirror, but the toothbrush tends to slip up my nose."

"It's weird," his roommate said. "You could spend a whole pandemic pretty much just with yourself and still not ever really know what you look like."

"Yeah… Only I'm here too." Rob said. He caught himself taking a cautionary step backward. His buddy was not usually this introspective.

Rob's roommate regarded him for a beat. "By this point in quarantine, you're sort of furniture." He laughed.

"Ouch," Rob said.

"No offense. I'm furniture too. Just a couple of ottomans."

Rob considered that. "I've always pictured myself as a glass front entertainment center."

Rob's roommate snapped off the light and headed to the living room. "All righty," he said.

"You okay?" Rob asked.

The answer was muffled in the folds of a "Live

Life Better. Read Books." Hoodie.

"Can we just go?" Rob asked. "We'll be late."

"Oh, is that today?" his roommate asked.

"Sure," Rob said. "We've been talking about it for weeks."

"But, I mean," Rob's roommate said, gesturing around. "Do you think it's safe?"

"We did a year in quarantine. The new protocols slowed things down. The vaccine is here. We can finally be…normal."

"Right," his roommate said. "Normal. What's that again?"

"People. Fresh air. The out of side. Let's go get it. It's waiting."

As Rob spoke, his roommate's head sank deeper into his hood. The muffled response, "If the out of side is really out of side, it can wait a little longer." Barely audible through the grey cotton.

"Seriously?" Rob said. "All we've talked about for months – "

"All YOU'VE talked about for months," the room corrected.

"You did too. Don't deny it," Rob said. He forced a chuckle, hoping to elicit one in response.

He didn't get it.

His roommate shrugged, flicked absently at the draw strings on his hood as he marched out to the living room.

Rob followed and pressed his point. "I think the old gang is meeting up for frolf and beers. Let's move."

The roommate pulled the draw strings of his hood tighter. "Maybe tomorrow." His face was barely visible.

Rob's eyes, though, were able to penetrate the fabric shield. "Take that hoodie off man," he said. It's like seventy-five outside." He glanced at the time on his phone and shifted a little irritably. His roommate noticed.

He of the hoodie sank deeper into the squooshy couch cushions. "You can't make me go."

Rob sighed. "I don't want to make you go. I want you to want to go."

"I'm sorry," his roommate said.

"Don't be sorry," Rob said. "Just come with me."

The hood drew closed more tightly. "I like it in here."

"But no one can see you," Rob pointed out.

"And the problem is….?"

"Well, if no one can see you, uh, you could get shot," Rob pointed out., grasping at weirdly violent straws. He wasn't good at this.

"Not if I stay here. Also, this isn't really convincing me to go out," his roommate said.

Rob looked at his phone again, acting as if hours

had passed since the last time he looked. "Well, is it cool if I go?"

Only hoodie man's nose was visible. "Of course. I'll go…next time."

"Sure," Rob said. "Okay." He got up and scooped his frolf stuff off the coffee table. Looking over his shoulder, he pointed to the table. "Your stuff is still here, if you want to catch up later. The usual spot."

"Sure," hoodie said.

Then Rob left.

And Hoodie didn't.

Someday he would. But not today.

Inspired by ATARI BYTES episode 245: ROBIN HOOD. Rob from the rich…and use it to buy books. Like this one! Or Misery Banana! Or Hell's Cereal! Or In the St. Nick of Time! You get the idea…

DANGLING THE CARROT

"Do we have any twine?" Sebastian asked as he shuffled into the living room.

Linda pulled off her earphones. "What?"

"Twine," Sebastian said. "Do we have any?"

"In the twine drawer," Linda said.

"Oh," Sebastian said. He half turned away, then turned back. "Wait. Which one is that?"

Linda sighed. "In the chest of drawers, Sebastian, between the 19th century Spanish stamp drawer and the uvula massager drawer. You know that."

"Oh, right," Sebastian said. He shuffled out of the room.

Linda put her headphones back on. Sebastian could be so thick sometimes. Good thing he was such a good pancake masseuse.

Linda had only just slid back into the warm, cozy melodies of classic Chumbawamba when Sebastian returned. Even without opening her eyes, she knew. It was his feral koala musk. That latest experiment had failed, but at least Sebastian could never hide from her.

"I told you where the twine was, Sebastian," she said, eyes shut.

"Yep. Got it." Sebastian held up a fistful of twine. "Do we have any carrots?"

Linda sighed, eyes still defiantly shut. She yelled over Dunstan Bruce's intense emoting. "In the refrigerator, of course."

"Which one?" He asked.

"The root vegetable refrigerator, obviously."

"Right," Sebastian said and shuffled out of the room.

Linda shook her head. Momma was gonna need some extra syrup tonight.

*****

Linda managed to get through Lawrence Welk's greatest reggae hits before Sebastian returned. "How about a staff?" he said.

Linda hit pause on the Greatest Hits for Cymbals. "Bo staff or quarter staff?"

Sebastian considered. "Bo staff."

"Basement closet. Behind the basket of shackles."

"Right," Sebastian said. He shuffled out of the room.

Linda watched her pancake man move away and wondered what she' do with her butter tonight.

*****

A short time later, the appliance love ballad Linda was enjoying was punctuated with a shattering of glass. She bolted upright, upsetting the chocolate-covered pretzel bowl resting on her stomach. Only then did she realize the glass breaking wasn't in her headphones. It was in her kitchen.

Feet asleep from hours of near inactivity, Linda hopped painfully into the kitchen. She discovered there that the already majestic, floor to ceiling view of a tree-filled valley below was now en-hanced with a cool, autumn breeze. The window was shattered.

With a groan, Sebastian pulled the Civil War era cannon on wheels back from the new opening he had created, glass grinding beneath its wheels.

"What the…?" Linda said.

"Oh, yeah," Sebastian said. "I borrowed your cannon. The catapult is broken."

Sebastian stepped around some shards and sat at the table, where he resumed tying long lengths of twine around uncut carrots.

"What are you doing?" Linda said.

Sebastian beamed, holding up one of his leashed root vegetables. "Hunting rabbits."

"Huh?" Linda said.

Sebastian took seven lengths of twine, each with a carrot on the end, and dangled them over the now wide-open window. He tied the ends of the twine to the cannon. "To catch the beast, you've got to have the best beast bait." He propped the broad sword and bo staff against the cannon, easily within reach should the combat degenerate to hand-to-paw.

"The beast?" Linda said.

"Yeah, the bunnies are amassing," Sebastian explained. Sort of.

"Bunnies?"

"Yep," Sebastian said. "Hand me the TNT."

"We're out."

"Oh, yeah," Sebastian said. "Dang it." He dragged a kitchen chair up to the broken window and sat, peering out into the valley.

"Tell me you're not spying on … bunnies," Linda said.

"Trust me," Sebastian said. "They're coming."

"That's…" Linda said. "That's stupid."

"You want the saber or broadsword?" Sebastian said. "The cannon fire should disperse a lot of 'em. But we'll still have to go hand to paw with the ones that get through."

"I can't even right now," Linda said, starting to leave.

"Oh, shoot," Sebastian said. "I forgot the boiling oil. I really prefer sesame. I'll be right back. Keep watch, ok?" Sebastian shuffled out of the room.

Linda could not believe any of this. What a dip-shit. Good thing pancake man was good with his berries. She stepped to the broken window and looked out over the edge. She'd always loved this view. She wondered how long the window would be boarded up before Sebastian came up with the cash to fix it.

Dumbass.

And that's when the ten-foot-tall eastern cotton-tail rabbit leapt up from the much-vaunted valley below and separated Linda's head from her shoul-ders. It even ate the headphones then hopped back down into its bunny crater. On the upside, for hours afterward, the bunny's farts had a Tuvan throat singing soundtrack.

Sebastian shuffled back in, pushing the pot of sesame oil on wheels. "I know I messed up the carpet. I'll take care of it," he started to say, then he glanced up to see the remains of Linda making the kitchen look much worse than anything he had done in the living room.

"Oh. Well, never mind then."

Inspired by ATARI BYTES episode 246: BUGS BUNNY. And carrots. They're good for the eyes, you know.

BAD POETRY CORNER:

THE DUKES OF HAZARDS

An ode to all those really good at screwing us over…

So many of us in our lives

Moving through life is the goal, man!

Trying to keep things light.

Keep stuff from hitting the fan.

We treat folks with respect.

Look out for fellow humans.

Protect health – land, air and soul

We're just doin' the best we can.

And then there are the others…

Some specialize at stirring up trouble.

Excel at sewing chaos and anger and doubt

Belittle and cajole and scorn

If you object, they'll chew you out.

Hypocrite much….?

Crown princes of chaos? Nah…

Common folk , except they're loud whiners.

But give them a bit of power…

Royal pains in our asses set the world on fire.

We'll call them dukes of hazards

Covid's a cakewalk.

Everything is conspiracy.

Climate change? What's that?

With little evidence for us to see.

The dukes surrounded by princes

Who spread hate and dubious facts.

The more they shout, the more believed.

But the one who laughs best laughs last.

They say we solved racism already.

Stop bugging me about health care.

No money for the jobless.

But plenty for companies. That's fair.

Politics is hazardous. See a duke and you're
tempted to put up your dukes. But here's the
thing…

Not all cops are bad, but some are.

Being rich isn't evil; neither is being poor

The way to stop riots is not quelling protests

Be willing to listen, or there's the door.

Dukes won't negotiate.

Calls for compromise fall on deaf ears.

We should all want what's best.

Even if we need to kick dukes in the rear.

I guess what I'm saying is – and it's tiring to have
to do so – and you know already, but here it is…

VOTE!

Inspired by ATARI BYTES episode 247: THE DUKES OF HAZZARD. Yes, this is the second story with the "just vote" message. But, you know, it's kind of important.

ALL OVER BUT THE SCREAMING

The great gust of wind nearly tipped the diminutive woman over. She clung to the tree trunk with long, thin arms, only letting go to wrap those arms around the man's frail body as he pitched forward out of the tree. With a bit more strength and just a few moments more, they might have been safe – for now - in their treetop shelter. But it wasn't to be. Not ever again.

She laid the man gently on the ground. Looking up through bare branches, the dying sun was swathed again in darkening clouds. She wished she understood what was happening, but also feared that understanding. Just as all humans always had to some extent.

Her mate groaned and shuddered as a cold front swept through. For warmth, she covered his naked body with her own.

He tried to grin at her reassuringly even as a rivulet of blood trickled from his mouth. She had a vague sense that once humans had been able to prevent the dying. But no more. The old magic, the med-I-nic was no more.

He didn't have a name. Neither did she. Names
required families, societal structure, language,
all of which had died as the Earth began to fade.
Societies fracture over time under economic pressure, political disagreement, race and cultural
disputes. Over time groups of people splinter. It's
slow, starting with a little more than a thing on
social media that makes us shake our heads today.
That discord slides into hostility and then political
movements. And then, like everything else that
seems important today, it turns to nothing. Lack-
ing anything to really believe in, identity becomes
lost.

All of which is to say she knew not what to call
this man before her, had no words for her love,
but love him she did.

He rolled over, coughed a gurgling cough and
was still. The two would not mate and bear young
now.

This was it. The Earth would die.

The scream that erupted from the woman's tiny
frame was swallowed in the roar of the Earth
cracking and breaking beneath her feet.

Desperate to be anywhere else, but no idea how to get there, she clambered up a small hill and looked into the valley below. There was no one there, of course. And there never would be again. The living become the dead and the dead wash away; consumed by water, flame or beast. This is how the Earth dies. Not in a war. Not in an epic space battle. Just one person at a time.

The woman sat and cried. But the crying quickly turned to anger. She didn't know much of humanity's ages old dimly lit history; the unwillingness to back down even from catastrophes of their own making. She didn't know about the wars that went too long, the environment tortured and protected in endless cycles, the illnesses that ravaged societies, were conquered then flared again in another form. She didn't know how the humans fought back, even as they fought each other...until finally they couldn't fight anymore.

She knew none of that. But a fire still burned within as hot as the fire that routinely gutted the forests around her. Her love was dead. She knew that. And that was enough to propel her. If this was the end, and surely it was, she decided, she would not go out just sitting here.

And so, she stood, walked, stumbled, and rose again. Propelled to walk during the day by the chill that enveloped the land and warmed at night by lava flows miles away. And this she would do forever if necessary.

However long forever was.

Inspired by ATARI BYTES episode 248: THE EARTH DIES SCREAMING. Because we're good at screaming.

CHUCK WAGON, THE
ANACHRONISTIC COWBOY

Spurs on worn boots that are caked with mud and worse jangled across the thankfully scratch-resistant laminate flooring. The thirty-something trio at the bar were socially distant from each other, but heavily engaged in conversation and didn't notice the stranger sitting at the other end of the bar.

A small poof of dust billowed forth as the stranger parked his ten-gallon hat on the stool next to him.

The bartender turned from her receipts, smiled and raised her face mask. She gestured at her face. "Sir. Could you please?"

The stranger smiled back. "Well, ma'am, if I cover my face with my bandana, I'm liable to get shot for robbin' the pine city stage."

The bartender laughed. "What? Did you just walk out of Red Dead Redemption?" the bartender asked.

"No," the stranger said, nonplussed. "Pine City."

"All right then," the bartender said. "What can I get you?"

"Whiskey," the stranger said. "Leave the bottle."

The bartender laughed harder at that. "Funny."

The stranger just grinned, bemused.

As the bartender set the stranger up with something off the top shelf, the stranger weighed a small bag of gold in one calloused hand, considering how much this drink was worth. Well, it wasn't sarsaparilla.

"Ma'am," the stranger said. "I'm Chuck Wagon. Pleased to make your acquaintance."

"Brittany," the bartender said.

Chuck Wagon tapped his brow as if doffing a cap. "Well, you're a right pretty filly, ma'am."

"Easy, friend," Brittany said. "No swipin' right here. I just pour the drinks."

Chuck had no idea what she meant, but he did enjoy drinks. "I'll drink to that," he said and tossed back a shot. He gestured for another.

As Brittany poured, one of the trio of thirty-some-things across the bar noticed Chuck Wagon and stroked his auburn beard self-consciously, envious of the stranger's luxuriant facial hair. "Hey, man," Lance called over. "What's your beard care regimen? Is it castor oil? Looks like castor oil. You use a derma roller?"

The eyes within the heads of Lance's friends, only recently bathing in the pleasant effects of gin, rolled mightily upward.

"Seriously," Lance persisted. "What's your secret? I like a lot of onions and hot chilis."

"Well, sir," Chuck Wagon said. "Every morning, I get outta my bunk, feed the horses and dunk my head in the horse trough. Then I go on about my day."

Chuck's bemused glare never wavered. Lance didn't quite know what to do.

Lance's friend Kennedy considered this. "You got a permit for in-town horses? My sister has one for chickens."

Chuck sipped his drink. A man dressed in cowboy gear, but all in black – he was like the stranger's shadow - approached the corner of the bar several stools away from Chuck. He regarded Chuck suspiciously, then said loudly. "Hey, is that a gun, mister? Gun! Gun!."

Bartender Brittany took a step. With a tremble, she said, "Um, we don't uh,"

Chuck barely moved. "My holster's empty, pard-ner. I know when to check my guns at the door."

Brittan leaned over the bar, satisfied herself this was true and refilled Chuck's glass.

The man in black sneered. "Feel a little vulnerable, do you?" he said.

"Nope," Chuck said, focused on his drink. "Do you?"

"No," the man in black said, sitting down next to Chuck. "I'll always be a step ahead of you."

Kennedy whispered to Lance. "What is happening right now?"

Chuck glanced at the man in black, then gestured toward the front window of the bar. "The dark is towering outside. You best be going."

The man in black regarded the stranger for a moment, perhaps considering his next move, perhaps considering Chuck's next move. Then he gathered up his change and started to walk away.

"See you 'round, pardner," Chuck called.

"Not if I see you first," the man in black said as he exited. "And I will."

Chuck shook his head.

"You know him?" Brittany asked.

"No," Chuck said. "And yes."

"Um..."

"Say, ma'am," Chuck said. "You got any hoe cakes?"

Brittany was a bit taken aback. "Excuse me?"

"You know...johnnycakes? Corn pancakes?"

"Oh. Yeah, no, we don't serve that. We do have loaded nachos."

"That'll do fine," Chuck said.

The platter of cheesy goodness was huge. "No way I can fit all this into my saddlebags," Chuck said. "Join me, young'uns."

It took a minute for Lance, Kennedy and Bryan to realize Chuck was talking about them. Bryan wasn't excited about this- he wasn't good with new people, nor was he particularly good with people he already knew. But the three of them did join Chuck Wagon at the feeding trough, as it were.

Before long, the three friends got Chuck out on the dance floor, impressed by his ability to square dance to Harry Styles.

As the tumbleweeds…er, tumbled …through the bar, night became day and Brittany grabbed her broom. Chuck Wagon, the anachronistic cowboy, handed the piano player a bag of gold dust and headed out onto the dusty trail. The piano player, it turned out was actually a truck driver making an early morning swizzle stick delivery, but no matter.

As the sun rose high in the sky, Chuck Wagon mounted his steed and galloped into whatever lie ahead. In his case, being featured in no fewer than a dozen viral videos.

Oh well, he reckoned, a viral video couldn't be any worse than rattlesnake venom, could it?

Inspired by ATARI BYTES episode 249: CHASE THE CHUCK WAGON and, let's say, nachos with beard oil..

CORPORATE AIR RAIDERS

Ted Calhoun stepped out onto the porch of his ranch-style, rent-to-own house, side-stepping the missing boards. He knew he really should talk to the owner, Kent, snotty kid that he was, about that. In Ted's day, slumlords like Kent would have been easy prey for a savvy land developer. Bull-doze the shacks and put up something useful.

But here Ted was; in a shack of his own. A guy Ted's age couldn't afford a fall. So he would talk to Kent tonight. He'd be nice; nice as he could muster. Kent was already doing him a favor; cutting Ted a good deal when he got out of prison.

With a groan, Ted lowered himself into the seat of his old Volvo and headed to work. He always knew he'd work 'till he dropped, but on chilly mornings well into his golden years, there were days he wondered just how close that day was.

The car rolled over 180,000 miles as Ted came to a stop in the faculty parking lot. He watched his cracked loafers as he went up the steps of Byron Dunkle High School on arthritic knees.

How he, Ted Calhoun, ended up here was a mystery. A mixture of luck, senior citizen charm and a series of called-in favors mostly. Some days, he regretted it, to be honest. Most days he didn't.

Ted straightened his wrinkled tie and swung open the door to his classroom just as sophomore Destiny Williams did a backflip over Eddie Steele and crashed into the small desk that constituted his office these days, pretty much wiping his coffee cup and other meager possessions to the floor.

Yep, some days he regretted his decision more than others.

"People," Ted Calhoun said. "Wrangle yourselves into your desks." He sighed and waited for peace to regain foothold. Once, he'd lead hundreds who shuddered a bit when he approached and would do whatever he asked. Now, he had a class of thirty who might quit talking for as long as two or three minutes at a time.

Ted picked up a marker and wrote in large letters on the whiteboard: CORPORATIONS. "Anyone know what a corporation is?"

"It's that game where you use tweezers to pull the little plastic leg bone out of the patient," said Kyle Miles, grinning as his eyes never broke contact with his phone.

"That's Operation, not Corporation, dumbass," his buddy behind him said.

"Oh, right," Kyle said, then turned back to Ted. "You mean the legal way of forming a group of people into one company that can buy and sell stuff and make contracts and stuff like that just like a person?"

The rest of the class applauded. Kye wore an expression conveying he was used to that.

"Very succinct," Ted said. "You really were listening yesterday." He looked out over the nonplussed classroom. "The advent of the corporation," Ted said, "ushered in a new era of business that would usher in a new age where power and money reigned." He paused for effect, but had little.

"But can anyone tell me who Kirk Kerkorian is?"

Ted asked, pressing ahead.

No one could.

"Carl Icahn?" Ted said.

No one.

"How about T. Boone Pickens."

The name got a laugh, but not recognition.

"Sir James Goldsmith," Ted said.

"My dad likes to listen to Sir Paul McCartney," Eliza said. "Whoever that is."

"Not quite the same thing," Ted said. "I actually met Paul a couple time. But that's a story for another time. No, these people were all powerful wealthy men who – "

"Patriarchy!" Kyle said.

"Well, the business world was different then, I

grant you," Ted said. "Corporations were powerful drivers of the economy. They employed so
many people. Provided goods and services. But
sometimes they got TOO powerful. Then it was
time for an elite, smart, dedicated men…"

"And only men," Kelly said.

"Frequently, yes," Ted acknowledged. "They were
called…" he paused and scribbled on the white
board in bold, block letters: CORPORATE RAID-
ERS." He tapped the board. "Anyone know what
these are?"

"Football team," suggested someone.

"Nineteen eighties hair band," said another.

"You're thinking of Paul Revere and the Raiders," Ted said. "Good stuff." They weren't actually
a hair band, but Ted knew these kids wouldn't
know the difference and he wanted to move on.

There was a collective shrug.

"Corporate raiders were people or groups of
people who would seek out vulnerable corporations, buy up shares of their stock to get control of
the businesses, then sell all or part of the compa-

nies for a profit."

"Like a lion takes down the slowest wildebeest in the pack," Kyle said.

"Well put," Ted agreed.

"That's pretty creepy," Kelly said.

"Sometimes," Ted said, nodding. "But history forgets how some of these raiders were heroes. Stepping in to prevent the evil that can corrupt those in power. Defense contractors. Pharmaceutical companies. Even food processors. All were vulnerable to being exploited by people who cared only about money. The eighties is already known as the "me" decade. The mantra "greed is good" and all that. But how much worse would it have been if the raiders hadn't swooped in to break up the monopolies before they broke up the country. Literally, sometimes, for, you see, there was an elite group of heroes called – "

Ted turned back to the whiteboard and inserted a carat between 'corporate" and "raiders" and wrote the word "AIR" above it.

"'Corporate air raiders'?" Kelly said, incredulous. "What's that?"

"A mighty and secretive force of corporate leaders

dedicated to the belief that business is good, that earning money is okay, but that one should not do so with trickery or deceit or in a way that exploits the good will of ordinary workers."

"But greed is good," Kyle pointed out. "You said it yourself."

"I said that's what a lot of people thought back then. But not everyone. Not the corporate air raiders. They kept greed at bay."

"How?" Kelly asked. "Give us an example." She wasn't buying any of this, but sensed a time-wasting yarn might be coming; a good bridge to sophomore lunch period.

But Ted wasn't biting. "That's confidential," Ted said. "Part of the air raiders deal with the government. The raiders do their work quietly. The government provides the funding for jet packs and stock buys. Anyway – "

The class woke up. "Jet packs?" several of them said.

"Of course," Ted said. "How else were the air raiders to get from Manhattan to Los Angeles to stop a takeover before the close of stock trading for the day? The raiders glide in, subdue the guards at a given corporation known to be planning a bad merger or release an unsafe product or whatever and remove the corrupt CEO. Then they work the stock deal in their favor and put the corporation in question back on the straight and narrow. Simple really. Now, who can explain corporate mergers?"

The class, though, was still stuck on the jet packs. They didn't buy his Iron Man wannabe stories about learning to fly; buzzing Yankee Stadium in jet packs and three piece and all that. But it was a good enough time killer until cinnamon rolls in the lunch room.

As the kids filed out of the classroom, one of them said, "Hey, Mr. Calhoun, tomorrow can you tell us about how Spider-Man solved the Great Depression?"

Ted Calhoun sat alone in his classroom reflecting on his life choices. Teaching was hard, man. These kids, they were so smart, but there was so much they didn't know. He wasn't sure he'd ever been all that smart, but he'd learned a lot. Not all of his choices were great – see the prison stay referenced earlier – but he knew who he was. That was something at least. He was a teacher. These kids, smart as they were, they didn't understand what the world they were going into had waiting for them. Corporations driving governments. Governments dictating people.

Ted stepped slowly to the closet at the back of the

classroom and unlocked the door, which opened with a creak. With a soft thrum, the jet pack hovered there, straining against its tether, waiting to be called into action.

Ted was a teacher yes, but the way the world was going, perhaps he'd be much more again one day soon.

Inspired by ATARI BYTES episode 250: AIR RAIDERS. I don't...I don't know where this one came from.

BAD POETRY CORNER:

I'M SO FULL

I'm so full.

Stuffed to the gills with Covid cookies.

Can't go out candy.

I'd eat a salad, but the world is icky..

I'm so full.

Why'd we think sourdough was a good choice?

Or curbside burritos?

Plans to get in shape were just white noise.

I'm so full.

The election is over, but not really over.

Whining and grandstands undermine the system.

Such a bad move to disrespect the voter

I'm so full.

Trump screams, "Stop counting!"

Everyone else screams, "Keep counting!"

That burbling sound is blood pressure mounting.

I'm so full.

Trump not all wrong. It is "Covid, Covid Covid".

But unlike movies or books or creepy dark rooms.

This is a real fright; don't discount the dead.

I'm so full.

Stupid fights over masks.

Screams of "Socialism!" by those who've never
cracked a book.

Next bear to poke? Afraid to ask.

I'm so full.

If you voted, that vote counts.

When children get mad at board games, they quit

No presidential maturity; not even an ounce.

I'm so full

Social media breaks to recharge

Myspace was never like this.

I got mail, AOL? Livin' large!

I'm so full.

So much to do; so much to see.

Brain so tired; feet are too.

Compulsively suck in all that's before me.

Come on, 2021! (Unless you're gonna suck worse…)

Inspired by ATARI BYTES episode 251: TAZ, I guess. Mostly, though, inspired by the dumpster fire that was 2020.

ENTERING SHEILA:

A STEVE STETSON, 1980s SUPERSPY,

ADVENTURE

With a massive grinding of gears and splintering of wood, the dump truck smashed through the barrier outside the county administration building and rolled to a stop. A few white envelopes fluttered out the back.

Commander Maddie Grimm stepped out of the building, adjusting her faux fur hat against the bracing Election Day chill. "You found the missing ballots?" she said, her voice a mix of relief and incredulity.

Secret agent Steve Stetson bounded lightly from the cab of the dump truck with a twinkle and a smirk.

"What? No," he said. "These are parking tickets and paternity test results. Gotta stop using the 'guess we ran outta gas' bit on my dates."

Commander Grimm deducted the dump truck rental fee from Stetson's paycheck.

QUEUE AWESOME STETSON SPY THEME HERE

Deep within Secret Operations Headquarters, Commander Maddie Grimm drummed the fingers of one hand on her desk while she tapped the intercom button with a finger on the other hand. "Ms. Carlyle, is Stetson there yet?"

"He's coming right now," she replied.

"Yeah, he is," Stetson's voice said over the intercom.

A moment later, the door to Grimm's office swung open. "Greetings, Commander," Stetson said. You're looking especially surly this morning. Mind if I sit?" He parked himself in the wing-back chair opposite the still open office door. All the better to avoid surprise entries; a survival tip learned by a man often at odds with angry husbands and boyfriends. And the occasional super-villain. But mostly the angry boyfriends.

Stetson poured himself a cup of tea from the pot on the table next to the chair. "You're out of sugar cubes," he said as he plunked eight of them into his porcelain cup. "Now, then," he said, "what brings me here today?"

"S.H.E.I.L.A.," Commander Maddie Grimm said.

"I swear, I wasn't with her," Stetson said.

"Not that Sheila," Grimm said. "She underwent selective memory wipe. Has no idea who you are."

"Well, which Sheila?"

The door to Grimm's office swung closed, revealing a tall man in a dark suit and darker disposition
had been standing behind it. "THIS S.H.E.I.L.A."

"I think I'd remember you, Sheila," Stetson said.
He gave the stranger a once-over. "Yes, indeed,
Sheila."

The stranger approached Stetson, handed him a
large three-ringed binder, turned on his heel to
stand at attention behind Commander Grimm's
chair. His expression never changed.

"You must be really good at freeze tag," Stetson
said.

"Stetson," Grimm said. "That is the operations
manual for your next assignment. We need you to
get inside S.H.E.I.L.A."

"Yeah, you do."

"S.H.E.I.L.A. is the Smirk's Hidden Empire of
Land and Air

"SMIRK!" Stetson said, toppling his tea cup as he stood. The shadowy figure behind Maddie Grimm was not pleased.

"It's just my resting face, Stetson," Grimm said.

"Was that…was that a joke?" Stetson said.

Grimm's face didn't move. "Yes," she said.

"I thought I destroyed SMIRK years ago," Stetson said.

"So did we," Grimm said.

"I knew you didn't," the shadowy figure said.

SMIRK was the organization run by supervillain Hans Hansley. The letters in SMIRK don't really stand for anything, Hansley just likes the sound of it. SMIRK. The acronym was the creation of Maddie Grimm's dark-suited aide.

A few years before this day in Grimm's office, Stetson dropped Hensley from a helicopter into a volcano. It was, Ingrid Johnson's 7th grade science project, but the vinegar in the fake lava really stung. Ingrid took third on her project, but won the "Junior Spy" Award from the Department of Secret Operations.

"So, Hansley is alive?" Stetson said.

"That's what we need you to find out," Grimm said. "That and you need to disarm the new super weapon."

"What super weapon?"

"Read the binder," said the dark-suited one.

"It's in the binder, Stetson," Maddie Grimm said.

"Well, then," Stetson said, throwing the binder over his shoulder. "Guess I'll just be surprised then."

*****

Eighteen hours later, thanks to Secret Operations mission assistants who knew where to drop him off, Stetson emerged in scuba gear from a sewage pipe deep within the bowels – ha! – of SMIRK. It was gross, sure, but the stealth approach was always the most effective in Stetson's experience.

That was when he was clubbed over the head.

When he came to, Stetson was chained spread-eagle on a steel table. He opened his eyes to the sight – the chicken-pot-pie-scented blur really – of a woman's face parked mere inches from his own. Her nose alone, he thought, spanned from ear to ear.

"Sheila?" Stetson croaked, parched. "Is that you?"

"It's Tamara," the woman said, backlit by the sodium light above. She stood up straight – she had to be seven feet tall – and punched Stetson soundly in the face.

When Stetson regained consciousness, three eyes peered into his. Tamara owned two of them. The third was the glowing red sight on a massive laser. With a grin, Tamara pressed the buttons on a remote keypad and adjusted the laser so that it pointed directly at Stetson's 'nads.

"Seriously?" Stetson said. "Trying to scare me? Do you really expect me to talk?

"No, Mr. Stetson. I expect you to fry." Tamara said.

"I hate that," Stetson responded. "When people say, 'time to fry' or 'you're gonna fry' from, like, lightning or lasers or something. I mean, you can burn or scorch. But you need oil to fry."

Tamara gestured to the laser. "Oh, this isn't for you. We use this to crack walnuts."

"Sounds about right," Stetson said.

"This, Mr. Stetson, is for you." Tamara pressed a button on her controller. The steel decking beneath the table holding Stetson in place slid open, revealing a paper machete volcano filled with boiling oil.

"Much better," Stetson said.

Stetson sensed another presence in the room. "We don't much like infiltrators," a creaky, old voice said. With the dull clang of a cane banging on the steel decking, the charred visage that used to be Hans Hensley came into view.

"We meet again, Mr. Stetson," Hensley said.

"I'd swear a puff of smoke just came out of your mouth," Stetson said. "How'd you survive the volcano?"

"Hatred, Mr. Stetson," Hensley said. "With pure hatred, you can survive anything."

"You're…welcome?" Stetson said.

"Do you know what I hate most, Stetson?" Hensley said.

"This oughta be good."

"Infiltrators," Hensley said.

"I prefer to think of it as party crashing," Stetson said.

"This is my domain," Hensley said.

Tamara pointedly cleared her throat.

"Our domain," Hensley corrected. "But the walnut laser is mine."

"Whatever," Tamara said.

"I think perhaps it's time to crack a few walnuts," Hensley said.

"Indeed," Tamara said, tapping at her controller. Were those fangs? Stetson was pretty sure he saw fangs.

Stetson stared intently as the laser warmed up, a little trickle of sweat pooled on his brow. Steady… steady.

At the precise instant the laser discharged, Stetson tossed a fistful of sugar cubes he'd swiped from Maddie Grimm's tea service into the path of the laser. The cubes were disintegrated, sending grains of sugar into his captors eyes, momentarily blinding them.

Unable to see what she was doing, Tamara's fingers on the laser controller sent the beam wild. One laser pulse cut down Tamara and another ricocheted off the wall and cut through the metal clasp holding one of Stetson's arms. As Tamara collapsed lifeless, cutting off the laser as well, Stetson managed to undo the manacles on him, thanks to a lifetime of bondage fantasies.

Hans Hensley skittered down a corridor. Stetson could surely catch the old man, but he had a mission to complete. That remaining unpunched spot on his spy loyalty card said so.

Helpfully, the schematics for Hensley's super weapon were on the table by the SMIRK headquarters front entrance along with Hensley's sunglasses, hovercraft keys and half a pack of Life Savers spearmint candies. (WE'D LIKE TO TAKE A MOMENT TO WELCOME OUR NEWEST SPONSER: LIFE-SAVERS)

Stetson scooped up the plans, the keys and the Life Savers – his mouth was still a bit dry. He turned to bolt out the main entrance to the hidden lair as S.H.E.I.L.A. started to explode taking the whole secret fortress with it because that's what secret fortresses do at the end of the movie.

"STETSON!" Hensley shrieked from an adjacent hallway.

Stetson turned, smirked, fittingly enough, and waved to his arch enemy. "Thanks for the Life Savers brand rolled candies," he said just as the roof caved in on Hans Hensley.

Moments later, Stetson was speeding across open water on the hovercraft, the secret fortress sinking beneath the waves behind him.

Commander Maddie Grimm came up portside on a jet ski, faux fur hat fluttering in the sea breeze, as Stetson waived the weapon schematics like sema-phore flags. Grimm climbed aboard the hovercraft and took the plans from Stetson.

"Hey, Commander," Stetson said. "Wanna suck my life saver?" He held up the half roll. "We could do that thing where we each chew a lifesaver, then kiss and make sparks."

Grimm took the roll and threw it in the ocean.

"Do you hate science, Commander?" Stetson said.

"You're an idiot," Grimm said.

COOL EIGHTIES STETSON END THEME HERE

Inspired by ATARI BYTES episode 252: INFIL-TRATE and the much beloved, if often question-able, pop culture of the eighties.

FELLOWSHIP OF THE STRING

The beginning of the end of their rope came for the members of The Tangled Cable…er 'cabal' during a meeting of the leaders of each of the cabal's stores. They sold string, chain and other implements of binding. They and ONLY they. Any new upstart in the neighborhood – say a paper-clip purveyor or Velcro brand strip distributor – would find itself tangled in a twisted knot of pain and regret.

If you needed something contained, collected, bound or bundled in this town, you used rope or chain or twine purchased from the cabal. No arguments.

Due to the recent abrupt closure of End of the Line, the leaders of the various bindings and binding accessory sellers needed to redivide the territory and find new customers. "End of the Line" had been in the neighborhood since the beginning of the line, ironically, and now that they were gone, some people needed to be reminded that if you need to tie something down, you best KNOT go elsewhere.

But before the twine whined, high level discussions must be had among the members of the cable…er cabal.

The leaders of the Tangled Cable…er Cabal wove their way through the roped off corridors in the basement underneath The Fellowship of the String, a local purveyor of the finest kite string, twine and other binding materials.

Fellowship of the String's owner Lenny McTigh, a reed-thin, lanky man in wire rim glasses, called the meeting to order.

Chain of Fools store owner Chet led the group to their seats at the table, huffing with the exertion of moving his large physique across an empty room.

Chet was an intimidating heavy, but his loyalty couldn't be broken. "Let's go, let's go," he said.

"We don't have time for this," Kate, the owner of Knotts Landing said. "We need to be in our own stores untangling the mess the market is in." Kate fidgeted constantly with "magic" kit unbreakable knot things people put in little kids' Christmas stockings.

"Now, now," Chet responded. "The finest chains are forged in fire,"

"Yeah yeah…" Kate said. "How many chains you sold in the last year?"

Chet huffed, but said nothing.

"People," Lenny McTigh said from the head of the table. "We find ourselves as businesses in a bit of a Gordian knot."

Saul from Stringer Things snorted at that. "Strung up by our own self-confidence, if you ask me. The string market is dangling by a thread. We should have seen it coming, what with all the loosening of morals and norms and bundles. When's the last time a publisher threw tied up bundles of newspapers on the newsies' porches to be delivered?"

"Um, 1934, I think," said Kate.

A nervous-looking newcomer in sunglasses slowly slipped into the room unobserved; each step seemingly reluctant, as if being pulled back into the stairway. He sat in a corner, watching the proceedings.

"Point is," Saul continued, "The market for tying things is being pulled out from under us by Velcro brand fasteners and apathy. People just leave stuff scattered all over."

"Madness," Chet grumbled.

"We don't need to get into that now," Lenny McTigh said. "I called you here today because I have new sales leads." He held up a folded piece of paper. "And by sales leads, you get that I mean people we can lasso into our cable, er cabal, right?"

The stranger in the corner sat up straighter, vibrating with tension.

Better Off Thread's owner, the well-dressed, though tightly-wound, Boris Banner, expressed what they were all thinking: "They'll hang us out to dry. They always do."

Chet started to say something about weakest links, but Banner wasn't done. "I know this cable, er cabal, is a patchwork of business and goals. But we're also a patchwork family, stitched together by a common purpose: to tie the world again."

"And make money," Chet said.

"Yeah, that too," Kate said.

Boris Banner shook his head sadly "Coming apart at the seams this cable is…er this cabal is."

"Annnyyywayy," Lenny McTigh said. "Do you all want these leads or not?"

"Hurry up or I'll zip tie your privates to the leg of the table," Kate said.

"We sell cuffs for that," Chet commented.

"All right," Lenny McTigh said, unfolding the paper in his hand, "I have it on good authority – my brother who works in adhesives is dating this girl in the advertising department whose dog walker buys her leashes from – "

"Just get on with it," Saul groaned. "I left a bag of string cheese on my dashboard."

"Okay," Lenny McTigh said. "So, there's this new upstart called Upstart Kites opening in – "

At that moment, the sweaty stranger in the corner screamed, "Benton Bungeee!!!!" and, flung himself from his seat, bungee cord attached to his ankles. He snagged the paper with the leads from Lenny McTigh's hand and retracted into his seat. He then propelled himself backward toward the exit and was gone.

The members of the Tangled Cable, er cabal, looked around at each other in stunned disbelief. "Bungee cords," Chet said. "I hate 'em."

Boris Banner took a more philosophical approach. "Perhaps we should look on this as a wake-up call that the times are changing and that we must change with them."

The others considered this for a moment. Finally, Kate spoke for the group.

"Where are the zip ties?

Inspired by ATARI BYTES episode 253: FELLOW-SHIP OF THE RING: JOURNEY TO RIVENDELL. I believe I did tell you early on the stories generally don't have much to do with the games…

FLOORED

The elevator doors slid open on the ground floor of the VanHuffle Building and Constance took a moment to steady herself. She was a wee bit nauseous.

She would never admit this, of course. Constance had enough problems without giving her coworkers another thing to kid her about. She was the new kid in the shop, eager to prove herself. After college, she never expected to get to this point, but here she was and today was her big day to prove she could do the job. Constance shifted a bit awkwardly in boots that were a size too large. She waited.

The elevator doors started to close when a large, thin hand gently blocked the doors. As the doors retreated, another hand appeared holding a small cup of chain coffeehouse coffee. The hands were attached to Eddie, thirty-four. He wore a plaid coat and permanently tousled hair. He smiled apologetically at Constance.

"Sorry," he muttered and took a position to Constance's left, both staring up at the numbers overhead as the doors closed and the elevator launched.

Constance cleared her throat and took a mental self-evaluation. She was ready as she was ever gonna be. She plastered a smile on her face and turned to Eddie. "Hey, stranger. In the mood for some excitement?" she said. Except she said it in French.

When American English speaker Eddie nodded politely, but didn't respond, Constance assessed and recalibrated. "My friend," she said in English, "I can show you amazing things."

The elevator dinged and the doors slid open. "I'm good, thanks," Eddie said politely enough and skittered away to his appointment.

As the doors slid closed, Constance's smile crumbled. Why was this so hard? Why was it so hard to get a man to come with her? She looked deeply into the reflective surface of the elevator's back wall, smoothing the folds of her dress as she assessed that what she saw was in order. Clearly, she would have to be more aggressive.

*****

Later that day, Eddie exited his chiropractor's office on the fourth floor of the Salamander Building, a new spring in his step. He reached for elevator "down" button.

But Constance beat him to it. "Allow me," she

274

said.

"Hey," Eddie said, puzzled recognition dotting his face. "It's you from this morning."

"It's me," Constance said. "Small world, huh?"

"I guess," Eddie said, looking around in hope of there being another elevator. There was not.

"You know," Constance said. "I could make your world so much bigger."

"Um," Eddie said.

"Come with me, Eddie," Constance said, looking into his eyes. "Come with me now. We can come to paradise together." She took a step toward Eddie as he took a step back.

"How do you…? How do you know my name?" Eddie said.

"Because I need you, Eddie," Constance said. "You have no idea how much."

"Yeah…So…thanks?" Eddie said. "Think I'll take

the stairs." The adjustment he'd just gotten from Dr. Amul facilitated Eddie's quick exit to the stairway.

Constance sunk back against the wall and slid to the floor. The elevator dinged and the doors slid open as if mocking her. "Not now," she said, waving her arm irritably. The elevator doors slowly slid close.

Constance was running out of time. If she didn't turn Eddie's head and soon, she didn't want to think about what would happen.

******

The next night, Eddie checked into the Howell Hotel, Bismarck's premiere hotel for the discriminating traveler. He rode the elevator to the eighteenth floor, duffle over one shoulder, key card brandished in the hand of the other arm. He was so excited to be attending the yearly Morning Woodies Convention, a club for fans of nature and morning television talk shows. Beloved "Today Show" weatherman Al Roker was slated to give the keynote for the weekend and Eddie had only just arrived in time.

Eddie approached room 1801, the coveted next-to-the-elevator room, holding out his keycard. The door to 1803 swung open and Constance stepped out. Eddie might have squeaked a little.

"Hurry up and stick your thing in the slot," Constance said. She smiled the smile of someone in a hurry, but trying not to look like it.

Eddie dropped his keycard.

"Why are you following me?" Eddie said. Then, second-guessing himself since he'd never had a woman look for him once, much less seek him out more than once before, he said. "You are following me right?"

"I need you," Constance said. "I can show you a great time. Just get in the elevator with me and let's go. Sights. Sounds. Tastes and smells the likes of which you've never experienced await. Just come."

"Look lady," Eddie said, trying real hard to affect a macho voice. Macho? Macho, right? That's still a thing guys do? Do they call it something else now? Eddie took a shot. "You're nice. And cute. And weird. But I…I… Leave me alone."

Constance stood straighter and hit the call button on the elevator. "There are wonders to be seen that you can't imagine," she said. "Just look at this." She opened her robe.

Eddie's eyes widened at the sight and he bolted for the staircase. Eighteen flights would be nothing, thanks to Doctor Amul. Eddie figured he could hide out at the Hoda Kotb breakout session in the convention.

Back on the eighteenth floor, the belt of the robe dragged on the floor, at the ready to mop Constance's tears. She had failed. As if she didn't know this already, the little voice within told her so.

"You suck," a gravely, robotic voice said.

"I tried," Constance said.

"Whatever," Bowl said as the fourteen-inch tall robot emerged from Constance's ever-expanding navel and gently landed on his feet on the floor. Given where he resided, Constance would call him "Bowel" sometimes. He didn't think it was funny.

And today, especially, Bowl wasn't in a laughing mood. "The universe is still doomed."

Constance's navel slammed close as the elevator doors opened.

"Well, you could have said something," Constance said, petulantly. "I didn't want to bring you out. He ran away because of you, you know. Humans don't like bellybutton robots."

"Racists," the robot muttered.

Constance closed her robe, then opened it again when bellybutton robot Spiral unspooled from her navel and coiled to the floor.

"Darling," Spiral exclaimed.

"Spiral," Bowl said coldly.

There was tension there that the end of the universe didn't allow time to explore.

"So we didn't get Eddie. What do we do now?" Constance said.

The elevator car hadn't moved, much to the chagrin of the Morning Woodies on the lower floors. Bowl pointed to the back wall of the elevator which gave way to the vast expanse of time and space. And much of it was on fire. "What do we do? We watch it burn. That's what we do."

Constance and the two miniature robots considered this.

Suddenly Constance jumped.

"Is my brother Flatiron coming out?" Bowl said.

"No," Constance said, excited. "But I think the universe is saved."

Spiral bounced in anticipation. "How? How?"

"Easy," Constance said. "George Stephanopoulos is at this conference right?"

The robots nodded knowingly.

And the universe was saved.

Inspired by ATARI BYTES episode 254: ELEVA-TOR ACTION and possibly strong cold medicine.

SIREN'S ECHO

When other kids in that little Nebraska neighbor-hood were playing hopscotch, foursquare and, if you were those brainy twins on the corner, chess, eight-year-old Emily was drawing maps. She was tracking the movement of the German army across Europe. The green line was for the Germans because for some reason she always thought of the color green when she thought of Germany. Maybe 'cause they sound alike. Green. German. German. Green.

Blue was for America because blue was Emily's favorite color.

Anyway, Emily listened to Edward R. Murrow on the radio every night with her mom and her brother Cal – when he wasn't doing pushups to get in shape for the army. Their dad was fighting with the allies and Cal spent most of his time trying to convince the recruiter he was old enough to fight – even though Cal was fifteen and the whiskers on his face were as fine as the hair on Emily's favorite doll's head, and there was less of it.

"Daddy's rifle is taller than you," Emily told him.

"Shut up, fat-head," Cal would grumble and go back to doing jumping jacks.

Every night Murrow would report from the frontlines on where Albert Hitler was. It was Albert, right? Albert Hitler? Emily wasn't sure. Morrow would report and Emily would mark it on her map. She didn't know how far Nebraska was from Germany, but on her map…well, it didn't look that far. A few inches, really. It was just smart to be ready.

When he turned sixteen, Cal convinced that recruiter to sign him up. Their mother was pretty resigned to the reality, but Emily was pretty upset. "I don't want you to go away," she said through tears.

"It's no big deal," Cal said. "You've got your map. You'll always know where I am."

Emily looked at the map as if for confirmation. "How? What if you forget to write and tell me? You don't even like to do book reports." Emily couldn't believe anyone hated book reports.

Cal laughed, trying, and failing, to puff out his boy's chest. "Listen. Wherever the action is, I'll be there. Morrow will tell ya every night."

After Cal shipped out, Emily went right on marking in blue and green on her map where she guessed Cal or her dad and the enemy might be. It was like a game, sort of. Long distance hide and seek. London. Paris. Cherbourg. Amsterdam. Wherever the allies were on any given day, Emily guessed her brother and father were there. Whenever the allies gained back a bit of Europe, Emily cheered them on as if she was watching Cal play stickball in the street in front of their house.

For weeks, the map game went on. Then months. Emily's map filled with lines and circles in many colors. Sometimes, she put triangles around targets she personally hoped the allies would liberate, mostly because she liked how the names sounded. It was deadly serious, but also great fun in the way of a child's mind.

Then, one day, the balance between fun and serious wobbled.

Emily was startled out of bed early one morning by the piercing wail of the air raid siren. Disoriented, frightened, but practical, Midwesterners shuffled to the bomb shelters. Sitting in lantern light, Emily drew a big circle around her town, at least six times. This was it. The war was finally here.

The townsfolk waited a while in the near darkness with their lanterns for the world to end. And when nothing happened, went back to their daily lives.

Turned out Wes Bently, the local butcher, had set off the siren after seeing a plane fly over the town he didn't recognize.

Although Wes the Butcher was deposed as air raid warden by Stan the grocer, most of the townspeople laughed it off. That siren, though, the enormous sound of it, echoed in the dark, normally quiet parts of Emily's brain, the parts that usually allowed her to think about fun things or to sleep at night.

She stopped listening to Murrow. She knew that unlike her little town in Nebraska, Murrow really was where the enemy was. And that meant her brother and father were too.

Eventually, she stopped drawing on her map. She didn't want to look at it anymore.

The air raid sirens went off a few more times in her town during the war. But eventually, the war ended and families were reunited. Other families. Not Emily's. She was glad, in a way, that she didn't have her map anymore. If she didn't know where her dad and her brother ended up, then, well, they could be anywhere; maybe even about to walk through the front door.

But they never did.

The air raid siren's echo kept Emily company for years after. She need only to close her eyes and let her ears take over, tuned to where that cacophony lived.

Emily grew up and became a teacher. She taught third grade science and geography in the 1960s, occasionally interrupted by the old, familiar klaxon. It was the warning that it was time for the kids to practice hiding under their desks so that the Soviets' nuclear missiles wouldn't harm them. It was theater, to be sure, but at least they were doing their small part.

But for Emily, the klaxon was sometimes the Soviets, sometimes her little hometown's air raid siren. And sometimes it was the sound of her brother banging on a pot with a wooden spoon just to drive her crazy when they were kids.

"Why are you crying?" Eddie Muss, age nine, asked her one day after one of these "duck and cover" drills.

"Headache," Emily said, through a thin smile. "Just a headache."

Nothing came of those drills either. No one ever dropped a nuclear missile on Emily's students and, eventually, her school and all the others stopped doing the drills. For a long time after the last one, though, Emily would flinch whenever the bell rang signaling the end of a period or the end of the day.

Years went by and Emily lived on. Air raid drills and "duck and cover" drills went the way of hula hoops and land-line phones. Only occasionally did Emily jump or yelp when the fire alarm went off from, say, burnt meatloaf.

Eventually, though, a new enemy emerged. And Emily found herself drawing maps again. Graphs too. She liked graphs. She was much older now; just a retired teacher watching the world she'd known for so long come to make even less sense. Illness ravaged every country, every city. Every home, even, at least indirectly. Emily tried drawing the map of the illness's movement, but it quickly became evident that the map was pointless. The disease was everywhere.

Instead, Emily drew her graphs of new cases. And new deaths. She repeated the advice to wear masks and social distance to everyone who would listen and shouted it to the ones who wouldn't.

She marveled at how people's response to this enemy was so much different than the response to war during her youth. Some people quarantined themselves, of course. But so many, instead of hiding – metaphorically - in air raid shelters or under desks, went out into the path of the enemy, defying it instead of fearing it. What would it take to make them pay attention?

Emily wished Wes the butcher was still here with his trigger finger on the siren.

Inspired by ATARI BYTES episode 255: AIR RAID and a healthy dose of existential dread.

LAST STAND IN TOY TOWN

Milo Vestibule limped on one leg only slightly less arthritic than the other over to the small shop's front door and locked it. He turned the laminated WE ARE OPEN sign to "CLOSED" and pulled the little shade down over the window. This was hardly necessary, given how dingy the glass was. But routine is routine.

It was six p.m. Christmas Eve. Time to close up for the holiday.

Maybe time to close up for good.

Milo looked around the shop, the way people do in stories when they think about walking away from something. Dusty, custom built shelves lined the walls, filled with all manner of wooden toys: carved animals and dolls, trucks and trains, puzzle boxes and the occasional music box – though not many of that last. Milo's late wife Linda was the musician, not him. The songs made his natural melancholy droop into sadness. When Milo's wife was alive and Milo was just a grump making toys in his garage, Linda would paint the toys. But she died long ago. And the toys suffered for it.

Milo grunted and tossed his torn green apron behind the counter, realizing a fraction of a second too late this was the apron with the torn pocket. Nails and screws flew everywhere. Milo's response was not very Christmassy.

He should have thrown the apron out, but his great niece Holly had drawn a picture of a clown on it with fabric paint when she was little. Milo was a sentimental fool.

Where the sentimental part stopped and the fool part began depended on the day.

With a groan and more less than jolly language, Milo knelt to collect the scattered shrapnel. He wondered, only half kidding, if he would be able to stand again.

"I should close this damn place," Milo muttered with less finality than he would have hoped. "I'm too old for this." Making toys by hand was a young man's game. For a long time, he thought he couldn't stop because no young man was willing to do it.

Maybe it didn't matter that much. Maybe it wasn't worth it.

Why did he need a whole store? Certainly not for the money. Milo's needs were few and the store only broke even in a good month. Once, he'd been content making a few toys for Holly or the neighbor kids. He called them bribes to keep those rascals out of his yard.

Then one day years ago…he wasn't sure when; time being a slippery proposition when you get older. One day, he woke up from an intense dream he could remember vividly, but also not all. He'd lived a whole life in that dream. It was, he thought, a complicated life, but what life isn't? When he closed his eyes and thought about that other life, it was a bright, colorful life full of joy and obnoxious goodwill. He loved it …and re-membered none of it. Not really. All he knew was he awoke filled with an urge to spread his toy-making beyond that modest neighborhood. And so, his shop "Toy Town" was born.

Of course, he used to mix cold medicine and Jack Daniels so, his memory is a little spotty.

But now, there was trouble in toy town. The local economy was in the crapper and so…Bah, think about that later.

Milo stretched his arm, bad shoulder protesting, to retrieve a couple hex screws that rolled under the counter. A chain of unpleasantness occurred. As he rocked forward, he nicked the corner of the counter with his temple, cursed and felt the air sucked out of him. His heart squeezed into itself as if trying to produce a diamond. Milo blacked out and slumped forward on the floor.

In the next moment, or so it seemed, Kyle, a ten-year-old kid from the neighborhood, kicked gently at Milo's boot. Milo didn't respond. So Kyle said, "Hey, you got any airplanes yet?"

"What?" came the muffled grunt of the man still face down on the floor.

"You said you was gonna make some airplanes," Kyle said.

With an effort, Milo rolled onto his side, trying to remember the last few minutes. Hours? Days? Who the hell knew? "I think I'm dead," he said finally.

"Oh," Kyle said, distracted by some wooden turtles on the counter by Milo's seldom-used credit card reader. "Okay. So, no planes, then."

Milo sat up. The room spun and he puked.

"Eww," was all Kyle said.

Milo's breath was shallow. "Really," he said in a whisper. "I think I died."

"It's Christmas," Kyle said, as if the holiday was a shield against mortality.

"People die on Christmas, Kyle," Milo said. "That's just -"

Something caught Milo's not quite focused eye. "Hey, why are you all glittery?" He thought there might be wings too, but wasn't positive about that part.

Kyle shrugged. "It's Christmas," Kyle explained. "Duh."

"Have your ears always been pointy, Kyle?" Milo

asked.

Kyle didn't answer that. Instead, he said, "Hey, Milo, what do you want for Christmas?"

Milo chuckled darkly. "To not be dead."

"Is that really what you want?"

"What kind of question is that? Of course, I don't want to be dead."

"We just like to make sure," Kyle said. "The boss isn't the only one who checks twice."

"'The boss'," Milo said. "You mean God?"

Kyle thought that was very funny.

Kyle pushed a toy train engine back and forth a few seconds, double-checking that the axles allowed free wheel movement. When he was satisfied, he turned to Milo, smiling. "I've seen better ones where I'm from, but this…isn't bad."

"I'm so glad you approve," Milo said with an inflection. His increase in heart rate was not met with appreciation by his chest.

"You liked doing this, didn't you?"

"That particular train? I guess," Milo said. "But it takes money to drive the train." He coughed. It hurt. "And I think the train is pulling into the station."

Kyle picked up a wooden play, doing all sorts of maneuvers with it.

"Hope you made a big Christmas goose this year, Linda," Milo muttered. "'cause I'll be home for Christmas. You can plan on me."

Kyle regarded Milo carefully; looked at the man lying there. He looked at the shelves full of toys for kids all over town who needed them. Kids who would never know Milo Vestibule's name. Kyle grinned appreciatively, knowing how Milo liked his anonymity; a man who asked for nothing in return. It struck Kyle as very familiar.

Finally, Kyle looked at the man on the floor muttering to his dead wife.

Finally, Kyle pocketed the train on the shelf and said, "Okay, I think the boss has enough info."

Milo tried to stand, but decided it wasn't worth it. "What are you talking about?"

But Kyle was gone.

Milo was dizzy. He didn't know what was going to happen. And where did that kid go? Should he really be alone right now? Being dead and all? What did Kyle mean "the boss has enough info"?

When the bells rang out for Christmas Day, Milo got his answer.

Inspired by ATARI BYTES episode 256: TOYSHOP TROUBLE. The ending is purposely vague. Make of it what you will! (Also, if you want to spend more time with Milo, check out my novel IN THE ST. NICK OF TIME wherever you like to order your books!)